Mickey Braddock's Works Do

Graham Wilson

Mickey Braddock's Works Do
and other stories

Millrace

First published in Great Britain in 1999 by
Millrace
2a Leafield Road, Disley
Cheshire SK12 2JF

ISBN: 1 902173 04 X

Typeset in Baskerville BE Regular.
Printed and bound in Great Britain by
Bookcraft (Bath) Ltd, Midsomer Norton, Avon.

Contents

And time for all the works and days of hands
That lift and drop a question on your plate

T S Eliot: 'The Love Song of J Alfred Prufrock'

Mickey Braddock's Works Do

It was coming up to Christmas and the bar of the King Bill was between shifts. The debris of the property speculators was settling in the lag-end of the late afternoon and those who worked for a living had yet to arrive. In the midst of this vacuum stood, or rather leant, Mickey Braddock, smoking a large cigar still encased in its foil band. I didn't know Mickey particularly well at that time but there are certain rituals that have to be followed.

Hello, Mickey. What are you up to?

I am on my works do.

But I thought you were self-employed.

I am.

So, you're on a works do by yourself?

Yes.

This seemed something of a conversation stopper and I was vaguely trying to remember whether he was interested in football, when he continued:

I have a theory about this. Most people, generally speak-ing, who go on a works do, do it with the people they work with. Right?

I nodded at what appeared from any angle im-peccable logic.

Well, I go on my works do with people (at this point an all-embracing gesture to include whoever might be present) *I don't work with.*

I thought it would be tactless to point out that, given his terms of employment, he had little choice in the matter but, it being *inter alia* the season of good-will, felt I should make some contribution that might encourage.

So, that's your theory, eh?

Mickey was not a tall man and the angle between the body and the bar became more acute.

No (another attempted inhalation) *that's not my theory.*

I waited.

My theory. My theory is that life is like a works do.

I'm sure you're right, Mickey. I started to plan the available escape strategies.

Like a works do. Life. At the start everyone's up for it. You know, friendly, feeling good. Really looking forward to it. You're happy. Even if you don't score, there's always the crack. Then things start to go, you know...?

Awry?

That's right, things become wry, then it's usually, 'You got a problem, mate?' and it ends in a punch-up. The land-lord calls the police and you've finished up on the street.

Cast into Outer Darkness?

Yeah. Unless it's a summer do, of course. So (a further tobacco intermission before the circle was squared) *it's best to go to a do with people you don't work with.*

I had worked out by now that this particular Yule-tide celebration was not in its infancy, a fact that was confirmed by what, under the circumstances, was a spectacular pirouette and purposeful exit in the pro-verbial puff of smoke. After a brief exchange with a door which, to conform with fire regulations, had been recently altered to open outwards, he turned and delivered what he considered, no doubt, the tell-ing riposte,

Well, that's my theory and you're welcome to it.

and departed to experience the interesting phenom-enon of the interaction of fresh air and alcohol.

As I considered the implications of this cerebral gift, the bar started to fill up and I had the chance to examine the Dramatis Personae of Mr Braddock's Harlequinade. The congregation (not so much a cast list as a suicide pact) didn't surprise me as all the watering holes of the town seemed to be inhabited by people who looked and acted pretty much the same. Indeed, a newcomer to the town could be excused for assuming that the inhabitants stood still and the pubs moved round them. However, among the usual throng of leftovers and latch-lifters, I noticed that during my conversation with Mickey Braddock Big H had returned. Now, it is not wise to upset Big H, who has a propensity for violence matched only by a streak of sentimentality that would make Patience Strong blink. He was carrying what appeared to be a shoe-box which, when placed upon the bar, developed a locomotion of its own.

It's a rabbit, he announced to no one in particular. *I bought it for our Gemma.*

'Our Gemma' was Big H's daughter and in the fall-out of domestic violence and subsequent guilt he would attempt to rectify the situation by buying a present—not for his wife, which would mean a serious loss of face, but for his offspring. The present was more often than not an animal and most often a rabbit. As the purchase completed the expiation of the guilt, the unfortunate beast rarely found its way to the Big H residence and was usually retrieved by the cleaning-lady from under a lounge settee of the best room the next morning. If he was in a determined or excessively guilt-ridden mood, he would order a taxi and despatch the creature, as one would a pizza, to the bosom of the family. Rabbits, by and large, were no problem but incontinent puppies and, on one celebrated occasion, a carpet snake caused cleaners and taxi-drivers to draw the line, with Big H on one side and them, very firmly, on the other. Ultimatums were delivered by the management and he was left with no future alternative but to return the items to the pet shop whence they were bought.

The owner of this emporium was quick to realise the economic advantages of selling an item one day and having it available gratis for resale the next, but slower to see the gradual fading away of other customers every time Big H hove on the horizon. By the time the vendor had explained that he had no responsibility to refund the price—even taking into account the mental state of the purchaser which, he agreed, had precluded the formation of the 'necessary intention' demanded by English Law—the shop had emptied. The case was inevitably taken up by the resident macaw and in the end it was felt that the only solution was to sever any commercial relationship, *sine die*. Exactly what happened at that moment has always remained something of a mystery but the local paper's lead headline concerning Big H and the Parrot complied exactly with the definition of 'news' as prescribed by the erstwhile editor of *The New York Sun*.

This and the consequential magisterial proceedings, where the Defendant was bound over on condition that he did not enter a pet shop within a ten-mile radius of the town centre, not surprisingly caused a hiatus in Big H's zoological ambitions and it was therefore of unusual interest that a rabbit was present at all.

This is no ordinary rabbit. This, he paused significantly, *is a Manchester rabbit.*

The combination of Big H, a rabbit and a full train at rush hour was too much to assimilate so I just nodded in what I hoped was the appropriate manner, trying to give the impression that there was nothing more to be said which could add to the last remark.

Whether I was successful or not, I will never know because my informant saw in the reflection of the bar mirror the entry of Ant, Billy and Charlie. It was clear from his reaction that he was expecting them and that they were an integral part of his Rabbit Disposal Plan. No sooner had they sat down than, taking the box in partially outstretched hands in the manner of the haggis bearer on Burns' Night, he processed across the floor to the table in question. I recall the pre-recorded music was playing 'I've got you, Babe.'

It's a wedding present for Gemma.

[Probably a note of explanation is needed at this point. Ant was about to get married and was on what turned out to be a series of stag-a-rounds with his two best men. Those who have been following the tale carefully will say–Ah! Gemma. Daughter of Big H. Ant is about to become Big H's son-in-law–and they would be wrong. The only connection that the affianced Gemma had with Big H was the intensity of violence both could inflict if upset. But Big H was, as has been stated, a sentimental man and the happy appellative coincidence was sufficient to give his scheme a symmetry and satisfaction of its own.] As the priest at the altar of his own self-indulgence he reverently laid the box and its contents on the table before Ant and his two best men. I appreciate that 'two best' is a grammatical impossibility, but the reality was that Ant had a dilemma. If he chose Billy, he could not be sure that he would wake up in time to attend the service. If he chose Charlie, he could not be sure that he would see the ring again. Even restrained young ladies would baulk at 'With this pawn-ticket I thee wed'. As for Gemma... So Ant's solution was to have both: Billy as the custodian of the symbolic circle and Charlie as the alarm clock.

As a central element in the General Theory as proposed by Braddock, Charlie is worth some consideration because he is present in much that follows, if not in person, at least in spirit. He was a clever boy. Not only clever enough to pass his 11+ but also to realise that through studied indifference he could slowly sink through the system of academic streaming until he reached a level where he was not greatly inconvenienced by matters scholastic, unless it was to make a bob or two doing the homework of others. Even at school he had other plans and, although no student of economic theory, they focused around the redistribution of wealth, mainly in Charlie's direction. He was quick to realise that it is not the fool and his money that are soon parted but rather the snob. He left school at the earliest opportunity and before long developed an uncanny eye for the all-fur-coat-and-no-knickers brigade. The simplest clue, as he explained to me once, was the ostentatious car or cars parked permanently on the drive of a house when there was a garage that would house a good proportion of the Tank Corps.

An early sally was into the world of the local stockbroker belt that nestled in the comfortable arms of a superior golf club. He had bought a suitable suit and an appropriate tie and, leaving his overalled assistant in a van which supported a large extension ladder, walked courteously up the drive to the front door and rang the bell. He noticed that it played a tune, which was encouraging. When the lady of the house opened the door to a polite and not unattractive young man, her worst fears were allayed once she realised his visit was not evangelical but as a representative of the local authority. It appeared that there had been a complaint—no, he was not allowed to reveal the name—a complaint concerning unpleasant emissions from the area of one of the soil pipes. They were probably escaping from the soil stack. The detector van had confirmed that action was necessary. As she would no doubt be aware, under the regulations governed by the Health & Pollution Act 1897, as amended by the County Borough and Parish Act of 1952, he had no alternative but to take the appropriate action. There were two possible lines of investigation that might be followed. He could send a gang of men to dig out the drainage system which, of course, he was sure she realised, was the householder's responsibility from the public utility on the highway to the point where it reached the house (Charlie would at this juncture turn and appear to estimate the length and composition of the elegant sweeping drive) or she could adopt what, he had to admit, might only be a temporary measure of inserting a baffle in the stack itself. The baffle, which effectively breaks down the molecular structure, cost ten pounds and could be fitted immediately. He gestured in the direction of the van, whose bonnet and extension ladder were discreetly visible at the end of the drive. It would only take a few moments to fit and it would cause the minimum of fuss.

The vision of a gang of men loudly announcing their arrival to sort out hygienic aberrations and the fact that she would have to accept the blame when her husband was unable to park his car because of 'bloody motorway maintenance machinery cluttering up the bloody place' usually tipped the balance. Charlie made sure it was in order to bring the van up to the side of the house and made it clear that he would instruct his man as to the placing of the ladder to avoid damage to the tasteful exterior décor. The assistant would then ascend the ladder, with much show of unwrapping the prophylactic foil, only to descend and announce that, as this particular stack was a BS 207, he would have to use the latest model. This apparently was fortunate because, as Charlie explained, the new model was much more effective and the baffle could well last for years—it was, of course, one of the advantages of buying superior property. The new, improved model was produced from the back of the van and in no time at all the job was complete. However, there was sufficient opportunity for Charlie to compliment her on the garden, admire the parked sports car, accept the tenner and give assurances for the future with a shake of the hand that had the slightest suggestion of appreciative pressure. The van would then depart at an almost funereal pace down the gravelled drive and through the large wrought-iron gates. This procedure would continue throughout the day until the box of 2 doz. plastic pan scrubs bought at Woolworth's at 20p apiece finally ran out.

It was on one occasion, when Charlie was expressing his amazement that a man of my abilities should waste his time in gainless employment, that he confessed it was the ten pounds that he was really pleased about. At the time of the operation, it was not so much that you might be offered a cheque, but right to the wire of what someone is prepared to pay to get rid of a man who says you've got a smelly house. Of course, the real trick was to keep cost in line with inflation.

I was awoken from these Temps Perdus by the sight of the rabbit–which was by this time out of the box and sniffing the ashtray in a somewhat supercilious manner–and the realisation that the conversation on table number seven (the one by the bandit, luv) had developed into an argument. As Ant assumed he, or worse, his fiancée was being made the butt of some tasteless joke and Charlie could see no immediate commercial advantage, they had been less than enthusiastic. Consequently Big H had taken umbrage that his gift had been spurned. Billy appeared to be, and probably was, asleep. The man behind the bar was becoming apprehensive and even the best efforts of 'I've Got You Babe', which was now on its third cycle, were eclipsed by the rising tide of emotion and recrimination. The rabbit had found some remnants of a salad that was used to justify over-priced sandwiches.

I wasn't overconcerned. Big H was big but it was at least two and, if roused, three to one and even Ant realised that turning up at your wedding with severe facial injuries and a variety of limbs in plaster might remove the gloss from the occasion. It was merely a question of how the matter would be resolved without too much loss of face on either side. As I watched the stalemate unfold, I began to understand, rather sadly, that in this subset of a subset (and what was probably Braddock's Special Theory) Big H had had his day and Charlie Shearing was the shape of things to come. It took the sight of Half a Lager Joe waving in my direction to make me realise that these affairs were a little too much for this particular Philosopher

King and, after smiling at the most attractive girl in the room, I took my leave. It was only as the door closed behind me that I became vaguely aware that the unwitting guest of honour at Mickey Braddock's Works Do was also departing.

Mind you, I can't blame it. This place was far too provincial for a Manchester Rabbit.

Care in the Community

The Stewart House Hotel had seen its origins as a town residence built for a successful textile manufacturer. It had stood on the outskirts of rolling parkland that belonged to a local dignitary and, as such, had the advantage of extensive vistas without the irritation of expensive upkeep. Eventually, this seclusion fell victim to the owner's commercial success, a success which resulted in the building of terraced cottages to house the workers. These, inevitably, ribboned along the edges of the road that led to his house. At first, walls were erected and dogs bought but when the next batch of building came uncomfortably close, he gave up the unequal struggle and, having secured his knighthood, sold the premises to a brewery which was owned by his brother. What happened to the textile king is not officially recorded but it was rumoured that he bought a remote Scottish island on which he built a castle.

What happened to his house is more certain. It became a pub. There was a brief attempt to live up to the implication that was now emblazoned over the front door, but it soon regressed into the norm for the area—a pub for men—and became generally known, as far as can be ascertained without any deliberate irony, as the Stew.

Whether it is true of the textile industry in general, I don't know, but in this particular town the greater proportion of the workforce was women who, with their nimbler fingers and less demanding wage structures, proved irresistible to accountants and employers alike. The consequence was a large number of men with time on their hands and no obvious source of employment. The industrious set themselves up as Jobbing Builders or Bookies' Runners, but those with a more philosophical turn of mind spent their time in the pubs debating the nature of the Human Condition, a speculation only interrupted by the exponential complications of Turf Accountancy. Even the Jobbing Builders, with no official office of work other than a plastic bag of dismembered cigarette packets covered in a variety of figures (the introduction of VAT came as something of a shock), made the occasional foray to pick up casual labour and check on prices. Social change allowed off-course gambling and women in taprooms, but the Stew did not and, to the day when it was demolished to make way for a road that was never built, it remained as it had begun.

This halcyon state of affairs was on one occasion briefly threatened. It was a warm June afternoon when four young ladies, whose flimsiness of attire was matched only by the firmness of their form, breezed in, having tired of a nearby wedding. Removing neither hats nor gloves, they took over the pub and the pool table. They were surprised by the lack of Pimms and after thirty minutes breezed out. The effect was somewhat akin to a bank raid. Grown men pressed themselves against the wall, hoping that the affair would end as quickly as possible with the minimum of personal damage. In other pubs, as in other bank raids, there may have been those who would have chanced their arm, but not in the Stew.

But this was a rare ripple in the sea of male tranquillity. The norm was better exemplified by the sight of the landlord smashing his hand and a not inexpensive wristwatch against the side of the television set as he and his customers exhorted the long-odd tip received from the owner whom he'd met on holiday in Malta. This opportunity for early retirement seemed invariably to be thwarted by a horse ridden by an unprintable version of Lester Piggott.

And so, as the laws of demand and supply settled the rarely disturbed dust, the Stew had only two things that differentiated it from the scores of other establishments that propped up the town's equilibrium. It was the home of the highest staked card game and it acted as an extension to the local hospital.

Now, this hospital did not cater for our brave lads who, in honing their skills for the next South Atlantic Crusade, required medical attention for a variety of cuts and abrasions received in the early hours of Saturday morning. They had to go elsewhere. This depository had been first a workhouse, then a lunatic asylum. No planning permission was required for the change of use, as poverty, madness and sin were generally regarded as interchangeable terms. It still contained women, of course elderly, who had been incarcerated because they had conceived a child out of wedlock and who were now, to the relief of all, indisputably mad. In a later day and age there was

somewhat less censure, though there was still the re-
sidual prejudice (voiced in the main by outsiders) that
you don't build a factory unless the raw material is
close to hand, and part of this enlightenment was to
allow the suitable male inmates to be processed by
their guardians from the hospital to the Stew, where
all concerned could indulge in light refreshment. This
formed on certain days of the week a mottled com-
plement to the crocodile of prep school pupils who,
scarlet smart, passed on the other side.

The conversion from private to public house had
been done with the minimum of fuss. The original
ground floor consisted of a large entrance hall, tiled
in bold black and white squares, from which sprang
five rooms. One of these was converted into the dis-
pensary; the hall became the bar area and the rooms
remained rooms. The landlord and his family lived
upstairs. The conversion of the hospital was a much
more complex affair. When those responsible for the
health of the County realised, on one hand, that
money could be saved by reintegrating the patients
into the community and, on the other, could be made
by selling the grounds to property speculators, there
was considerable fuss. But the redundancies and plan-

ning applications went ahead and the objections eventually faltered and died away. The patients were dis-
tributed about the community and local house prices
rose in a most satisfactory manner. I am sure there
were some excellent schemes but the institutional-
ised are, by definition, creatures of habit and slowly,
one by one, they found their way back to the Stew.

They were in the main uncommunicative, if loyal,
and there were four in particular who were always to
be found. No sooner had the door opened than they
were to be seen, one in each of the four rooms. Each
had half a pint of mild and sat in such a position that
he had a clear view of the bar with its chequered
floor. Four rooks waiting for the game to develop.
Each had his distinct, unchanging pattern. Horace
would constantly rearrange the beer mats and ash-
trays, first on his table and then, in a series of lightning raids, those on the other tables in the room. Bert,
to avoid eye contact, would stare fixedly at the ceiling even when drinking his beer. Gordon, who sat
with his hands pressed to the table top, had the studied expression of a man who was about to make some
momentous decision and remained in that pose until a woman, presumably his mother, came in and

ordered him out. Len, whose incantations of real or perceived wrongs that he had suffered at the hands of society started as a scarcely audible mumble, then rose decibel by decibel as the day progressed until they reached a crescendo of concentrated abuse that he poured on the head of a certain Mrs Gladstone. When the bell rang for time he would immediately stop, straighten his tie, carefully place his cap on his head and with a gruff 'Good evening' step out into the night.

Others were more extrovert. Las Vegas Joe, who had an unexplained source of money, bought huge cigars and made imaginary phone calls for taxis to take him to the airport.

How can I possibly get to Vegas if they can't turn up in the next ten minutes? was his usual envoi and he would then slump into a chair, legs outstretched yet slack-limbed, as though the whole of the public transport system was in cahoots to deny him his simple pleasures.

However the star of the show was undoubtedly Stevie. Stevie was a kleptomaniac, not in the usual sense of stealing from Marks & Sparks things that you fancy, but as a sufferer from a compulsion to

'take care' of things he came across. Like the jack-
daw, the shinier the object the greater the attraction.
Those who knew him were careful to take elemen-
tary precautions to safeguard their property; those
who didn't, on being offered a light for their cigarette would remark that they also had a lighter of
that particular design and manufacture, only to find
that they hadn't. One of his favourite positions was
to sit just inside the doorway of the room adjacent to
the fruit machine in such a way that he was invisible
to the person who was operating it. It was an old-
fashioned machine and, if the player won, the coins
and nice shiny tokens would be disgorged into a
bucket-like tray with an opulent sounding rattle and
clatter. At this point Stevie's hand would make a
knight's move out of the room, round the corner
and skilfully scoop the pot. By and large, it was only
nuisance value, as he could be easily persuaded to
return the things he had been 'caring for' and any
impropriety was outweighed by the amusement it
afforded. The winner of the jackpot, flushed with success, would reach into the tray with one hand while
he continued to push the buttons with the other. The
search was at first nonchalantly confident, then a more

careful sweep of the length of the supposed cornuco-
pia culminated in a panicking grovel as he realised
that he would be unable to insert a token in time to
ensure the continuance of the latest run of good fortune. The search would then move from manual to
visual. The tray was clearly empty. What happened
next was an interesting revelation of character. The
timid glanced about on the floor, then gave it up as a
bad job. The violent seized the top of the machine
and tried to shake out their rightful deserts. The determined started an inch by inch search that culminated in them on their hands and knees, attempting
to peer into the stygian fastness that lay under the
machine. At this point, Stevie, if he was in a particularly 'caring' mood, would leave his post and offer
helpful bits of advice.

Apart from this idiosyncrasy, Stevie was a model
citizen. He had been around in the old days but had
seemed to enjoy trusty status: he did not have to take
part in the daily procession but appeared to come
and go much as he pleased. The only real blip on
this newfound treatment of the mentally infirm was
when he disappeared, having taken care of the keys
of the Dangerous Drugs Cupboard. Much rushing

around by those irresponsible and a temporary sus-
pension of privileges but, as Stevie said, you've got
to be careful not to leave keys lying around in locks:
you never know who might find them.

Amongst these peccadilloes, there was one which
became engrained in the mythology of the Stew and
even today is recounted by those who found their
world pulled down around their ears and had to seek
refuge amongst the alien corn. It so happened, on
this particular morning, that I was standing at the
bar chatting to a new and more sympathetic landlady when the door opened to admit a man of military bearing. After a glance round the virtually empty
rooms, he came to the bar and ordered a gin and
tonic, large. By the standards of the average denizen
of the Stew, he was smartly dressed, wearing a 'guards'
tie and a camel-hair coat. His shoes, although highly
polished, were besmeared with streaks of mud. It was
only when he raised his glass to drink that I noticed
that the underpart of his sleeve was covered in what
appeared to be a green stain. I have to confess that
he was not the sort I take to and his opening address
confirmed that he was the type of man who had his
suits 'built' and referred to his car as 'not a bad old

bus'. In fact, the main reason I drank in the Stew was to avoid him and his ilk.

Is there a phone, old boy? I need to find out the times of the trains to Leicester. Got to see the Tigers, don't you know. You a rugger man, old boy?

Although my experience of the game was limited to standing in the wind and rain, waiting to be flattened into the mud, I thought it simplest to nod.

Splendid! What's your Club?

(What a tangled web we weave.) I was explaining that I was sort of between Clubs when I was rescued by the landlady who offered to ring the station to check the time of the trains.

Splendid! Thank you! Will you have one yourself?

Having learnt from experience, I declined and after dispensing 'another drop of the old juniper juice', the landlady disappeared into the private quarters to make the call. This left the two of us alone in the bar. Once the door had closed, his whole demeanour changed. Where previously he had leant, almost casually, on the bar at an angle that encompassed both the landlady and myself, he now moved parallel to the counter and, staring fixedly ahead of him, spoke out of the side of his mouth.

Is she sound?

Sorry?

Sound! Is the girl sound?

I assured him that, to the best of my knowledge, she was.

Good. She won't be ringing the police then?

He took my bewilderment to indicate a negative and after glancing both ways continued, still staring at his reflection in the mirror at the back of the bar.

I've just come over the wall. Jumped ship. They tried to put me away but I've baled out. Over the wall, through the laburnums and the long grass of the Cricket Club. You a cricket man? Not my scene really. Nothing against them, mind. Leopard crawl—not as fit as I was. You never forget the old Army training. That's the problem nowadays—no National Service—never did anyone any harm.

I was about to mention the dead and maimed but thought better of it. I certainly didn't feel up to inventing regiments.

But can't miss the Tigers. Tigers' last game. Always go to the last game. Jonny Johnson and me have a few chin-chins.

I noticed that during this exchange his drinking arm had slowly risen to the extent that the glass was now poised permanently on his lips and his elbow was parallel with his nose, so that he appeared to be giving some (slightly valedictory) salute. The land-lady returned with the news that there was a train in ten minutes but he would have to change at Stoke and Birmingham. She had jotted the times down on a piece of paper. The station was no more than five minutes. If he went out of the back door and cut down the ginnel he would have time to spare. With a gra-cious salaam and a conspiratorial wink, he departed.

No sooner had the back door closed than the front door opened and admitted two policeman. They glanced into the four rooms and approached the bar. The younger of the two seemed to regard me with some suspicion. The older took charge.

Have you had a man in here? Probably wearing a light brown overcoat. Well spoken.

The landlady nodded and looked to me for con-firmation. The younger, whose demeanour stated that if I'm not Inspector by the time I'm thirty I'll swal-low my truncheon, turned in my direction.

Did he say where he was going?

Now he mightn't have been my sort but every-thing is relative and, if you come to think of it, he was one of us in a way—at least in the sense of them 'n 'uz. But no point in making a rod for your own back, so I gave them a bit but not much.

To watch a rugby match. He had to catch a train or something.

En passant, Stevie had come in clutching what appeared to be a small bunch of keys and was trying to attract my attention.

What match? What was the team called?

I dunno. It didn't have a proper name. Some sort of nickname. Some sort of animal with black and yellow stripes.

Comprehension dawned on the constable for whom now the CID beckoned.

Black and yellow! Wasps. It'll be Wasps, Sarge. They're at home to Bath. He'll be catching the London train.

Right, get in that car, lad. We'll just catch him.

Their exit was impeded by a figure standing outside the door, apparently checking some detail before entry. Any regular would have known that it was Mr Richardson, as he liked to be called, coppering-up and who, despite his appearance, was out of work and had been so for some time. But the sight of a bowler hat and a rolled umbrella was enough for the constable to assume that he couldn't just push past him as he had the recently arrived Stevie, who at this moment was explaining to me that if he had told them once, he had told them a thousand times about the dangers of leaving keys in locks. As they departed, I took Stevie by the elbow and propelled him towards the rear exit. I assured him that I knew he was only taking care of them but it would be much nicer if he and I went and had a pint at the King Bill and sorted things out from there.

What transpired was hearsay. It seemed that a somewhat less assured police constable rushed back into the bar, made a swift search of all the obvious surfaces and rushed out. With the imprecation 'You lost them, you start it' ringing in his ears, the ignition had been bypassed and the patrol car and its occupants arrived at the railway station to see the London train easing its way off the platform. But there was no real damage done, as it was a non-stop express and they could phone through to the lads at the Met to pick him up at Euston. The complacency illustrated by the U-turn that, in normal circumstances, would have been a candidate for a charge of dangerous driving might have been dented if they had bothered to notice that on the adjacent platform the stopping train was closing its doors on a slightly bedraggled but nevertheless distinguished looking gentleman who, on checking the times of the connections, had worked out that with a bit of luck he might just make kick-off.

The Funeral Directors

Two men, one who still had the remnants of the appearance of an individual who was used to being obeyed and another who might have been young enough to be his son, paused at the cemetery gates and, as was their habit, read the Latin inscription before passing through. The elder had grey, short-cropped hair and wore a black crombie overcoat. The other's coat was also black but the raglan sleeves served only to emphasise the rounded shoulders and a slightly hangdog appearance that was crowned with wispy fair hair. They traversed the Garden of Remembrance, nodding in the direction of the various plaques and plants as if they were old friends, which in a sense they were, and eventually reached the Chapel of Rest. In a picture-framed window were the services of the week, which they respectfully observed.

Cyril had fallen on hard times. As a young man,

although from humble beginnings, he had possessed a range of talents that guaranteed success at most of the things to which he had turned his hand. His problem was that he was not interested in the activity as such, merely whether he could do it or not. Once achieved, it was easily discarded. He had reached a position of eminence in the Local Authority at a ridiculously early age, only to abandon that career and join the Army. The applied structure suited him and he soon reached the rank of Major. However there was some problem relating to Mess Funds and military service ceased. This event closed the doors on orthodox employment and he drifted along amongst the litter of his money-making schemes which, even if initially successful, eventually petered out. As did, for the most part, his self-esteem and dignity.

In contrast Gordon, the younger of the two, came from a long and distinguished line of latch-lifters. His grandfather had learnt at an early age that it was the custom for Carters to be given a pint of beer at a reduced price. A service of which he availed himself by the simple expedient of stealing a Carter's whip, the established token of authenticity. His son and Gordon's father had a more inventive turn of mind.

In those days landlords prided themselves on their hospitality and when neighbouring pubs visited to play skittles or cards, free food was supplied in abundance. Gordon Senior made a careful catalogue of which pub served what food on which night, then sold copies of the Bill of Fayre at a penny apiece to visiting vagrants and the like. He ensured his weekly entertainment by visiting the Red Lion at 1.30 every Wednesday afternoon, where he bought half a pint of beer and sat at the table by the window overlooking the street. Here he had a good viewpoint to spot the crocodile that wended its way towards the local cinema. It was part of what then passed for care in the community that the harmless inmates of the local Institution were allowed, free of charge, to watch the afternoon matinée. As the straggled line passed the door of the pub, it was only a moment's work to finish his drink, ruffle his hair and, with a suitable drooping of the lower jaw, join not quite the end of the queue.

But times had changed and as the taxation laws were more forcefully applied and charitable acts had to have discernible return, the spare ribs and mutton broth were replaced with paper thin plastic ham sandwiches (strictly for the players only) and pay to view was the order of the day. It was in this hour of mutual need that Cyril and Gordon teamed up. The answer to their penury lay in funerals. There was always food and usually a deal to drink. As long as you nodded sympathetically and remembered the deceased well, you could find copious amounts of life-sustaining fluid and an abundance of vol-au-vents and sausage rolls. So, a regular inspection of the dearly departed was essential to glean the necessary information. Once a list of names had been gathered, it was fed into the network of their drinking acquaintances, so that a portfolio of background material could be garnered. Armed with this intelligence, it was no difficult matter to palm themselves off as old friends from the past. If appropriate, a suitable muster of military regalia would add verisimilitude:

It was so good of you, Major, to make the effort. I do hope you and your friend can come back to the house.

There were certain ground rules of engagement when choosing their silent benefactors. Cyril constantly reminded Gordon:

(a) They should be male—it was always tricky to try to establish a historical relationship with a member of the

opposite sex without raising eyebrows. And, in any event,
widows were more susceptible to commiserations followed
by flattery.

(b) They should have liked a drink—this would mean
that they had a circle of pubs and each would assume that
they were attached to another.

(c) They should have had relatives who did not know
them.

And certain strategies to be followed in the field:

Always shake hands with the bereaved. It is very diffi-
cult to accuse a man of improbity once you have shaken his
hand.

The town was an ideal size for this exercise. Large
enough to offer variety but not so large as to induce
hostility to strangers. Although the rise in crime meant
that folk no longer left their doors unlocked and on
the latch, they did in a metaphorical sense and the
habit of neighbours popping in uninvited and unannounced was still accepted, at least by the older generation.

Of course the crematorium was not the only source
of information. Hospital porters could act as intelligence agents and discreet enquiries amongst the
town's hostelry could produce useful lines of enquiry.

The experienced eye would pick out the emptied cigar tin marked 'Collection for John (Jack) Dixon', which would indicate the purchase of flowers for the funeral, as opposed to 'Collection for Rosie', which would indicate marriage or some other less terminal condition. For no more than the price of a half of mild, a contribution to the fund could justify an appropriate cross-examination of the landlord and the planting of the seed that 'they and Jack go back a long way.' Weddings and christenings also had food and drink as an attachment. But funerals were best. The circumstances made the deflection of potentially awkward questions easier to achieve, arrival and departure times could be the more accurately gauged and, as Cyril remarked:

The old-fashioned Christian values are still extant on these occasions.

To which Gordon, in not quite the non sequitur that it appeared, once added after an uncharacteristic amount of thought:

You know, it's the difference, Cyril, between scrounging and burglary. The burglar takes and gives nothing. Whereas the scrounger is a source of satisfaction to those that help him.

Cyril, who was of the 'God helps those that help themselves' school of action, considered this a little sanctimonious, but let it pass.

Sunday, as was right and proper, was their day of rest and recuperation. An interested observer would note that they appeared amongst a steady trickle of men wearing collars and ties who would stroll up to the narrow alley that ran alongside the Stew and look left and right before hastily disappearing into the darkness. The alley, of course, led to the back door of the public house and gentlemen used to accepting the morning libation at eleven o'clock on six days of the week felt it unreasonable that they should have to wait until the permitted hour of Sunday. So, when the front door was officially opened at midday to admit the law-abiding citizens, they found the bar full of those who felt that these particular regulations were best honoured in the breach.

The additional attraction was the profusion of card and domino games that took place during the afternoon. There were two rooms known respectively as the 'Tanner' room and the 'Five Bob' room. Fluctuations in the value of the pound made no difference to the basic premise, that is, you could win or lose

ten times as much in the latter as the former. The
'Tanner' room, as its name implied, was cheap and
cheerful. The games were played for modest stakes
and there were a variety of tables where schools
of Three Card Brag, Chase the Ace and Fives and
Threes operated. The games were conducted amongst
the usual obbligato of mild cheating—extra pegs
would be taken, ears would be scratched and what
appeared innocuous enquiries about the fortune of
the local Football Club passed information on key
cards. But, as everyone did it, all evened itself out
and justice was approximately done. Cyril and
Gordon generally frequented this room where, by
drinking moderately and playing the percentages,
they nearly always paid for their Sunday lunch and,
if there was a surfeit of foolish virgins, added a little
to The Pot.

The Pot, when it reached a certain point, was their
entrée to the 'Five Bob' room. Where the 'Tanner's'
door was always wide open and people wandered in
and out at will, the door to the Holy of Holies was
kept firmly shut. Only Maurice, who waited on,
opened and shut that door and was to be seen between games shuttling to and fro between it and the

bar, his elaborately extended quiff acting as a bowsprit to part those preventing access to his service area. Inside the room was the normal arrangement of tables and chairs but only one table housed the game. This was placed in the middle of the room and surrounded by four straight-backed chairs. The game was a form of partnered whist using the whole pack. The winner of the trick scored points according to the value of the cards taken. The points were then scored on a pegboard operated by a neutral referee, who also dealt. The essential tactic was to discard point-scoring cards into your partner's winning trick and to avoid doing so into your opponents'. Although this was a popular game in the region as a whole, the Stew had a particular variant–you pegged round the board twice, i.e. gained 120 points, but on the second round had to peg out exactly into an additional hole at the bottom of the board. The easiest scores to achieve in a single trick were five, nine and eleven, the hardest, by far, was one. The skill of the end game was to manipulate yourself into an easy winning position and to avoid at all costs landing in 'Dead-Man's Hole' needing a single point to clinch the game. A two, and particularly the deuce of Trumps, though not valuable in itself, was more often than not the card that turned the lock.

Whereas the games in the 'Tanner' might spill on throughout the afternoon until the last straggler had wandered off to reheat the beef and roast with its by now congealed gravy, there was a strict limit in the 'Five Bob'. Ten games and ten games only were played. If you were in at the start, you were expected to stay there. You placed the agreed sum on the card table and identified it with a personal marker. The dealer then dealt a card against each marker in turn until the four Jacks appeared; the holders of the four Jacks had the game. The stake money, worth two or three times the average weekly wage, was collected and formed the pot. It was at this point that negotiations began.

The holders of the Jacks would be subjected to severe pressure to sell the right to play for five to ten times the stake value. Those who had gambled in the hope of a quick return invariably did. Those who fancied their chances sat down at the table. Those with sense nodded in the direction of one of a small group of men who sat aloof and apart, smoking hand-rolled cigarettes and sipping halfs of mild. These were the professionals who, for a set fee, would play your hand. Cyril and Gordon, in the event of their winning a Jack, would sell if they were short, put up a jockey if funds allowed a flutter.

But the money on the table was a mere bagatelle to the real money. This consisted of the side-bets that were placed on the game. The Stew attracted big money and big money attracts bigger money. There was a group at the time with money to burn, Scrap Metal Merchants, Chinese Take Away Proprietors, the Sellers of Goods that Balanced on the Tightrope of Legality. All liked a bet but were not prepared to risk their social standing by frequenting the normal betting outlets such as the Stock Exchange. Of this group none was more enthusiatic than the Scrap Metal Merchant known, though not to his face, as Cruel Bob and the Purveyor of Countless Cartons of Chow Mein, Mr Lee. They would bet against each other on the outcome of each game. The initial sum was not known, though rumoured to at times have reached four figures, but it was clear that at the half-way point whoever was in the lead would taunt the other by signalling that he was prepared to lay odds if the stake was increased.

The set of ten games was half-way through when it was Gordon's turn to go to the table and lay their bet. He placed the money on the table alongside his marker, the lucky bus ticket. To Cyril's delight, a Jack appeared and the auction began. Gordon did not seem interested in selling and was obviously intending to use a jockey. The choice was his prerogative. Three of the sharp-faced men had already accepted the commission and were beginning to take their place at the table. Maurice had returned with the latest orders and change in sufficiently small denominations to ensure a tip. It was then Cyril realised that Gordon, too, had sat down. How many times had he told him?

The Golden Rule, Gordon, for God's sake. The Golden Rule is never play your Jack.

It was too late. He was sitting down at the main table at the Stew, the Stew on Sunday, and the audience stirred. Cyril could see that Cruel was not a happy man. He had won the last bet and protocol gave Mr Lee choice of partners. Mr Lee did not choose Gordon and friend. Unlike the 'Tanner', where non-players milled about, peering at people's hands and inhaling sharp intakes of breath, the 'Five Bob' room was an example of perfect decorum. Spectators sat in silence. The Dealer dealt, then, as each card was played, would identify it with the necessary commentary:

Spades are Trumps. Billy (or whoever it was) *to lead. Ace of Trumps–Three of Trumps–Four of Trumps–Six of Trumps. Ten scored. The lead still with Billy.*

And so on until towards the end of the game:

Seven scored. Billy requires five for out.

The game was about to start when Cyril looked again. Gordon sat studying his cards more in a mood of defiance than resolution. However, as with all matters of chance, there are days when things go right and this was one of those days for Gordon. The cards fell in such a manner that not only did he win trick after trick but his partner always had the suitable riposte to ensure the scoreboard kept ticking over. Once round the board and they led by a street. This was the moment when the side-betting traditionally stepped up a gear. Cruel, smiling in the direction of the Chinaman, lay first three fingers across the wrist of the other arm, followed by two. Three to one at double the agreed odds. Mr Lee spread his hand, fingers outstretched. He then folded three into his palm. If he was going to double the stake he wanted fives. Cruel looked at the ceiling, then at Eddie, Gordon's partner. Eddie was recognised as the shrewdest player in the Stew and that meant the County. Eddie looked at the hand that he had just been dealt and, for a second, his eyes seemed to half close. Cruel looked back at the ceiling, placed his outstretched hand on the table and nodded. Mr Lee took out a cigarette and then his wallet.

This hand was crucial. Eddie led and all fell into place. Even Cyril relaxed. Gordon had done all he had to. Play safe and let the professional pilot the game into the safe anchorage of the final hole. Cyril fell to calculating the final pot and converting it into double whiskys. But, for some reason which he could never explain, Gordon blew it. It was his lead and he played a Spade, which was currently Trumps. The next player, knowing that his partner had already discarded on Spades, played low. Eddie's eyes flashed up to look at Gordon, then back to his hand. He saw the look of excitement that often overtook the amateur when big money was at hand. He knew from experience that Gordon would try to rush to finish the game. He decided on balance that it would be safer if he took control by winning the trick and taking over the lead. The strategy carried a risk. If the fourth player had a deuce, the points won would put them in the Hole. The silence grew quieter. Eddie paused, then took the trick. Sure enough, the two of Diamonds duly appeared.

The effect was immediately apparent. The opposition, previously slouched, pulled itself to the edge of the chair. The Chinaman replaced his wallet and at last lit the cigarette he had been rolling between first finger and thumb. Cruel Bob started to sweat slightly and his eyes appeared to bulge. He stubbed out the freshly lit cigar with uncharacteristic petulance. The game, like the weather, had changed. Wherever God places the odds, it is not with the foolish and Gordon, in an attempt to rectify the situation, made error after error. Eddie could no longer second guess his intentions and the boat foundered in the harbour with the loss of all hands. Cyril was not happy. That Cruel had lost a deal of money was obvious by the way he wrenched out his cheque-book and spread his considerable bulk across the table as he began to write off his debts. Then, with a cross between a sob and a sigh, he seemed incapable of

continuing and slumped forward. Someone coughed
out of embarrassment. Maurice broke the habit of a
lifetime and allowed two empty glasses to clink together on the tray.

It was reported at the inquest that he had got no
further than writing the date, the payee and the sum
in figures. For the sake of propriety the actual amount
was never revealed but, even allowing for exaggera-
tion, it was agreed that it must have been a very expensive item that he was reputedly buying from Mr
Lee.

The sending off was, as to be expected, a flam-
boyant affair. The immediate family consisted of two
brothers, who barely tolerated each other, and their
two wives, who didn't. In their efforts to honour
Robert's wish that 'people should have a good time
when his turn came', each side proposed plan and
counterplan as to venue and the like. In an attempt
to reach a compromise, the arrangements were split
between them but the grieving had scarcely ceased
before disparaging remarks were being made about
the standard of catering and the disproportionate
amount of beer to wine. Cyril was just remarking to
Gordon how nice it was to be an official guest for a

change, when the younger brother's wife turned to her spouse and demanded to know how long he was prepared to stand there and let her be insulted by this trollop. The older brother came to his wife's aid and within moments fraternity had turned to fisti-cuffs. Glasses and sausage rolls flew in equally rich profusion and it was clear that the time had come for a tactical withdrawal. Cyril rescued a bottle of gin and what appeared to be a rather nice malt whisky and motioned Gordon to do likewise.

Nodding deferentially, they passed through the door as the groaning board gave way under the com-bined weight of by now a variety of bodies, operat-ing jointly and severally, and, at a respectful pace, they turned the corner to disappear down the street. Once clear, they quickened their step in the direc-tion of home.

You know, Gordon...

Gordon recognised the tone and looked into his friend's face, wondering what gem of wisdom would emanate on this occasion. Cyril removed the bottles from his poacher's pocket and started to place them for greater balanced comfort in each of the pouched side pockets of his overcoat.

You know, Gordon. Life is like the Great Games of Chance which, if we allow them, will always instruct and reveal. I hope you will realise from your recent experience that in Life, as in Cards—the malt whisky at last fell snugly into its Scottish woollen recess—*it always pays to save a two or two.*

The National Lottery Winner

J ohn Richardson was emptying the dishwasher when the phone rang. This produced the usual dilemma. Should he leave it ringing for his wife to answer, or should he answer it himself? If he left it, there would be much clattering downstairs and impatient opening and closing of doors, designed to register her disapproval of having to do three things at once. If he answered it, he would have to endure the various explanations with all their, by now, wearily barbed undertones.

Of course, it was unusual for John to answer the phone but he was...

in the process of changing jobs:

No, I don't think we'll be moving - we're so settled here;

on holiday:

We were going to go away, but there was so much to be done in the garden. Probably Madeira at the end of the season;

or just feeling a little out of sorts:

No, nothing serious. You know what these men are like. The first sign of a cold and they think that they are at death's door.

The truth—that he was a failure, that he couldn't get a job—had, at most costs, to be concealed. Of course Margaret felt bitter about it. She had not even the satisfaction of feeling that she had been tricked. She herself had made assumptions. That he would be the son of his father who had lived in a spacious detached residence with a walled garden and an abundance of rhododendron, who had sent his only son to what was considered a Good School, where he had learnt rather than understood the Classics, Shakespeare and approved Victorian Poetry. A man who had worked till he dropped to provide a life of style and class for his family. Yes, she had assumed that that was the direction of travel, not the cul-de-sac of semi-detacheds with their invariable dralon curtains and commonplace company cars. Goodness knows, she had attempted to burnish the image by joining the Inner Wheel and the Ladies' Committee of the local Conservative Party. But no matter how bright the smile or how ingenious the interpolation of a limited wardrobe, he knew that she knew, in her heart of hearts, that she was tarred with the same brush: he was a failure—she was the wife of one.

He consoled himself that, whether he answered it or not, he would soon escape. At eleven o'clock on each weekday, he went into the bedroom and put on his jacket. He would then go to the table beside his bed, count out and pocket the requisite sum of money for a pint and a half of bitter and, with a scarcely comprehensible muttering that he was off, walk rain or shine down the road, through the cemetery—that monument to Victorian optimism—and into the town centre. There he visited, depending on the day in the month, either the King Bill or the Stew. If there was an *a* in the month, he went to the King Bill on Monday, Wednesday and Friday, frequenting the Stew on Tuesday, Thursday and Saturday. If there was no *a* in the month, the rota was reversed. On Sunday he cut the grass and waxed over the rust on the car. He was secretly quite pleased with this arrangement. New Year, for instance, would symbolically herald a change of routine and he could see that the respective landlords were at a loss to explain why a man who, month by month, had steadfastly appeared on given days of the week, suddenly did not.

He went through the cemetery for at least two reasons. The first was to avoid a peculiar man-child who, in apparent contentment, spent his life sitting on a wall outside the hostel that cared for him. If he took the direct route to town he had to pass this particular place and no sooner had this latter-day Trabb's Boy spotted his approach than he would leap on to the pavement and march up and down his portion of the street, raising an imaginary bowler hat and swinging with some élan an equally invisible furled umbrella. Matters were worse if there were an audience of passers-by. The encephalitic would then fall in step behind him and, mimicking every movement, raise with greater flourish the imagined hat to all and sundry. This would continue to the next junction when, in the manner of a Drill Sergeant, the arm and its umbrella would be extended at full length and the prematurely wizened body and his platoon would wheel around the corner and out of sight.

The second reason was not so clear in his mind but had something to do with the gravestone. As he walked along the gravelled paths that crunched overloudly like footfalls in the nave of a church, apparent reproval for sins committed but as yet unannounced, the figure on the plinth came more clearly into focused view. At this time of the morning it often caught the sun and the marble of the cherubic child stood in pathetic relief against the background of evergreen. As the inscription on the chipped stone grew discernible, he would read for the thousandth time 'In Sacred Memory of Herbert (Sonny) Dear Son of Herbert and Amy', etc. He thought of the Japanese (it could have been Chinese) proposition that every man should in his life do five things—climb a mountain, plant a tree, write a book, father a son and something else which he had forgotten. Not that there was much chance of that. It had been made clear at the outset that chipped skirting-boards and jam on the carpet were not on the agenda.

Having arrived at, on this particular occasion, the King Bill, he paused before entering and, standing outside the glass inner door, carefully checked the money he had put in his pocket that morning. He had a morbid fear that he would ask for the additional half pint only to find that he had insufficient funds to pay for it. There was no doubt that his eyesight was failing and, in the comparative gloom of the bedroom, he might easily have mistaken a ten pence piece for a pound coin. It had happened once when the price of beer had risen without prior notice. Although it was easy enough to avoid the potential embarrassment by forsaking the second drink, it had produced another complication. It meant he had left the pub earlier than usual, and arrived home at a correspondingly earlier hour. This was interpreted as a reproach for dinner not being on the table and, for some considerable time after, was the subject of mock-injured enquiries concerning the punctuality of meal service.

Once in, having bought the first pint, he borrowed the *Mail* (the *Sun* in the Stew) and under the cover of the Stock Exchange section considered the ongoing problem. This was Mother. Not that Mother was a problem but her health, or comparative lack of it, had demanded a move into The Falling Leaves Nursing Home and her capital asset, the sale of the misleading house, was insufficient to generate enough income to meet the monthly nursing fees. It produced a good proportion but, month by month, the capital had been eaten into, stimulating the vicious circle of decreasing income and consequent further erosion. At the current rate, it would not be that long before the nest egg reached the level where even the Government accepted that enough was enough and allowed application for State Assistance. This would, in all probability, mean a move from The Falling Leaves to a less expensive establishment and, although this would cause obvious problems and tax his wife's powers of explanatory camouflage to their limit, it would—by definition—disappear with time.

It was not that which worried him but the effect it had on his Master Plan. That was the cause for real concern. The pension plans that he put into operation in better times would allow the two of them to live at a modest but acceptable standard and, more importantly, would be more than enough for one. His Idea had been that when Mother died, he would sell the house, pocket the proceeds and disappear. Most of his mornings were spent in planning this manoeuvre to the last detail. As often as he dared, he would visit the local library to pore over maps looking for the ideal remote and peaceful spot—the North of Scotland or the South of Ireland perhaps. He knew there would be a difficulty in finding a place to live.

He couldn't do any advance planning in that direction. The letter from Miss Brown at the library had been more than enough without Estate Agents' brochures landing on the breakfast table. He would change his name to Jack Dixon (he was pleased at that touch) and spend the rest of his life free from the telephone and comparisons with Madge's Tom.

Madge says that Tom isn't sure whether to take up the place on the Board of that company I mentioned to you. She says he feels that he must preserve the quality space in his life.

He had decided he would probably take up fishing and try to develop the image of the country gentleman. Perhaps buy a dog. The idea of trading in Margaret for a dog amused him, but it was not something he would exploit. The letter that he would leave, by now so rehearsed that he had it by heart, would not be vindictive, merely factually polite, giving details of domestic and financial provision—the courteous guest taking his leave in proper order.

That would be the end of it, except that on the anniversary of his departure he would travel by first class rail to a town that he had never previously visited, have a meal at the nicest restaurant that he could find, search the antique shops for a piece of 'exorbitant' china and then, as a combination of Birthday and Christmas, add one to his collection. Finally, he would send a postcard hoping she was well.

But the Master Plan had lost its crystalline simplicity. It had become clouded by a variety of strategies aimed at resolving the declining financial situation. The most extravagant was, using his Power of Attorney, to withdraw what remained of the capital—still a substantial amount—and, taking it into a Manchester casino, place the lot on the roulette table at even money odds. If he won, the problem was solved; if he lost, the inevitability of the State Nursery would be reached sooner rather than later. Although he was excited by the idea, he knew that he would never go through with it. There were too many questions. Would the Casino accept such a large sum of money? If he won, would he be robbed or cheated? If he lost, what would he say to Margaret and what would she say to him? Kipling's was a nobly romantic notion, but even he would see the current ironic absurdities of keeping mum. If Literature was to provide an insight, it was that the slings and arrows and sea of troubles seemed about equally poised. It was, he decided,

prudent to pursue a more conservative course and to
this end he would cut short his visits to Mother and
slip into the library to read what he could on *Personal
Finance and the Way to Prosper,* or whatever other com-
panion volumes Miss Brown had so thoughtfully put
to one side.

In fact, it was in a tome of that title that he found
it. It must have been used as a bookmark and, even
though he knew it must be where he put it, he could
not resist frightening himself by tentatively placing
his fingers, at first carefully and then vigorously, into
one waistcoat pocket, then the other before coming
into contact with and taking out the folded piece of
paper. Flattening the creases, he read yet again the
numbers 13 08 38 16 09 40 LD. Try as he might, he
could not recall the exact sequence of his reactions.
At first, he must have been struck by the coincidence
that the numbers reflected absolutely the birthdays
of himself and his wife. Then there was the echo:

*Isn't that funny? The numbers—you know the numbers
on the Lottery—are the same as our birthdays.*

At the time he had nodded, taking little notice.
But when was it? A week? Two? Three? The ticket
was dated two Saturdays past. It certainly had not

been claimed. It had been in all the papers and on television.

The next day, instead of reading the paper in his corner seat, he had stood at the bar of the Stew and, in what he hoped was a casually disinterested manner, quizzed the landlord about the National Lottery. He explained that a cousin had bought a lottery ticket that might have won a small prize. At a moment's notice, the said cousin had been ordered to the States for six months (you know what these big companies are like—they pay five plus figure salaries and assume that you are at their beck and call) and he had been asked to check it out. The landlord explained that if he took it to the kiosk in the shopping mall they would tell him if his cousin (was there a slight hesitation at that point or had he imagined it?) had won or not. If it was a small amount it would be paid there and then.

Would it make any difference if it were a larger amount?

The landlord took him through the procedure of writing to the Head Office and was surprised when the movement to fill the glass with the assumed half pint was prevented by a firm shake of the hand. John Richardson made his way to the mall and, after some time, finally attracted the attention and services of the kiosk proprietor. There came to him a moment of quiet satisfaction when the young man on the other side of the counter realised what he had been given. What had previously been regarded as an unnecessary interruption in the business of trying to chat up the blonde in the next stall, some boring old fogey who didn't know his Instant from his Lotto, now assumed a somewhat different light. When all is said and done, six and a half million pounds is quite a lot of money.

And so, it had seemed at first sight that all his problems were solved, but a few days' thought showed that they were not. On the one hand, the money had to be claimed in the immediate future or the prize would lapse. On the other, the Master Plan could not be put into operation while Mother was still with us. It wasn't simply a case of take the money and run. He had observed from his perusal of the Stew's journalistic offering that big winners, despite assurances of anonymity, were relentlessly hounded down by the Press. If he were identified all would be lost. At best, houses would be bought, motor cars replaced. At worst, the interrogation:

I never knew you bought Lottery Tickets. How much did you spend? Not that it matters now. But it's the principle of the thing. I met Madge in town and she was thrilled. She did hope we would remember the Cause.

The exact nature of the Cause had always eluded him, but he suspected that it gave a sense of gratification to the giver and the burden of gratitude to the receiver. The Cause and Madge had for long been the benchmark by which Margaret measured social acceptability and she would positively preen at the thought of being in that particular driving seat:

I do hope, Madge dear, that this little something will go some way to alleviate…

Maybe he could get someone to deal with the matter on his behalf. What did the Scots call it? A Factor?

I wonder if you would be prepared to act as my Factor in this matter? It will require the utmost discretion and I expect a number of other transactions in the future.

He practised the speech, trying to sound matter-of-fact but not offhand. Decisions had to made. Decisions that would change all for the good or for the alternative that he'd rather not consider.

However, it could be put off no longer; the decision

had to be made. It was clear that she hadn't heard or wasn't going to answer. He wiped his hand carefully on his apron and walked along the corridor into the hall. The phone continued to demand his immediate, undivided attention. He picked up the receiver.

Hello. This is 79432.

Is that Mr Richardson?

Yes.

I am terribly sorry, Mr Richardson. This is the Assistant Matron of The Falling Leaves Nursing Home and I'm afraid we have some bad news. Your Mother, sadly, passed away in the night. I can assure you she suffered no pain.

Thank you.

He placed the receiver back on its stand and stood for a moment in silent contemplation. Almost without knowing it, the first finger and thumb of his right hand slipped into a waistcoat pocket. They first withdrew, then rolled into a ball, a slightly stiffened and somewhat creased oblong piece of paper.

Do as you would be done by

Lord Chesterfield: *Letters to his Son*

An Offer You Can Scarcely Refuse

Although named on his delivery into this world as Charlie—there was a confusion over the exact spelling when the matter was broached at the centre that registers Births amongst the other obsequies of humanity—his business cards bore the legend *Charles A St J Shearing* in what he considered a particularly tasteful embossed copper-coloured script. Charlie had found out early in life that women in the right sort of mind, rather than of a certain age, were the best touch and, as they ran a finger across the slightly raised surface, they would disguise the connection they were making between this and a similar tactile experience with this most personable young man, by asking what the *A* and, indeed, the *St J* stood for. He would explain that the Augustus reflected his mother's genuine, if slightly risqué, interest in classical antiquity and the St John (of course pronounced correctly, as he was sure she was aware) was to please an uncle—a slight smile at this point—who was not only a great admirer of his mother but also had a passion for the affairs of the Tory Party in the early eighteenth century.

At this particular twist, or possibly turn, in his career path, Charlie was flogging burglar alarms. There was no doubt that the entrepreneurial spirit spread by recent political régimes had caught on and the God helps those who help themselves view of life had spread to those who helped themselves to property belonging to others. This, in turn, spawned the manufacture of preventative measures and, as these prophylactic shields were punctured by those who had undertaken an education rather than schooling, systems became redundant and new models became available. It seemed that this self-feeding foison would be never-ending and, provided that you made or sold anti-theft devices, you couldn't go wrong. But, as the stockpile of stolen car radios threatened to overtop the European Butter Mountain and people inexplicably refused to replace stolen goods with updated alternatives, keen students of Keynesian economics realised that the bottom was about to fall out of the market. Charlie had observed these runes of mural graphology and realised the need to diversify. To be caught with all your eggs in one basket, regardless of the position of your trousers, was not Charlie's style. Charlie was more of the dodge and weave than the take it on the chin school and prided himself on it.

Thus he had come round to considering antiques. There had been a certain moment in time when there had been a dispute in his negotiating a deal over an automobile as to the exact meaning of 'depriving the owner permanently thereof' and he had been forced to spend a short period of time incarcerated until the matter was resolved. Not only did it arrive at a satisfactory solution, with sincere apologies all round, but he had learnt from the co-habitee of his cell the rudiments of antique dealing. His erstwhile acquaintance had some distinction as a furniture restorer but, to the dismay of the owners, had for no obvious reason taken to furniture deprivation. Never one to waste an opportunity, Charlie had gleaned the fundamentals of the game. The basic strategy was to persuade the client that the genuine article was in fact a reproduction and, as such, was relatively worthless. The tactics varied. Perhaps the machine-turned screw was the most elegant. Here the dealer removed the screw from, for example, a hinge and held up for inspection a previously palmed screw whose perfection of thread demonstrated that it must have been post-industrial revolution, thus marking the piece as relatively modern. If it had been as old as the owner thought, the screw would have been hand-turned, with all the consequent irregularities. The original screw was replaced. A suitable offer was made and a profit was registered. However, Charlie's vanity favoured the double bluff. This consisted of overbidding for a relatively worthless object and then, as an afterthought, offering a low price for the desired artefact. He had found that the average punter was so excited at getting an unforeseen windfall on the former that he rarely stopped to consider the true worth of the latter.

And so, on his visit to Mrs Robinson, his main aim was to sell the anti-theft device that his company advertised in the local paper but, having seen the address, he had every intention of keeping his eyes open in the hope of advancing his secondary career. His client was middle-aged and muddle-classed, living as she did in the no longer most fashionable district in the area. Charlie knew that this was, nevertheless, where the real money lay, rather than Stockworth, where the mortgage repayments swallowed up the spare cash and where the new money had certainly not inherited much in the way of breeding, let alone antiques. She was apparently a widow and fortyish but careful control of the calories and the tonsurial tint had kept her, as they say, on the right side. As Charlie was between wives he was at his effusive best because, as he said to his mates in the King Bill, you never know in this world, you never know. There's more than one way of getting what you want out of a client.

Charlie had all the patter. Figures showed that a house without a VSD (Visible Security Device) was ten times more likely to be broken into than one with a VSD. The trouble with the visible device was that it had to be visible, visible enough for the average ill-educated intruder to notice, and therefore it had to be garish. He was sure—at this point he allowed his eye to wander over the discreet make-up, well-fitted but modest dress and absence of ornamentation—that garish was not a word that applied to her and that a purple box with a fork of orange lightning would hardly enhance the honeysuckle that he had so much admired when he had been admitted through the front door. Mrs Robinson intimated that she did not, on the other hand, wish to be considered dull.

At this point he paused to examine a porcelain figurine and commented that he had an aged aunt who had an interest in such things. No, what she required was the MSS (PP). The reason for the Maximum Security was, he explained, because of the appendage of Police Presence. The Alarm, as such, was no longer effective. They went off so often that they had been accepted as an irritating but inevitable part of urban life. Burglary was no longer a science, more a matter of smash and grab, with the emphasis on the smash. Mrs Robinson glanced around the room with its variety of frail objects and winced. Charlie carefully replaced the figurine that he had been holding and explained the strategy. The game was double bluff. There was an element of risk but the potential outcome outweighed the possibility of failure. The external security should be no more than a Yale lock. This the intruder could spring with any piece of plastic and entry would be effected with the minimum of damage. However, within a few moments a sensor, if not deactivated, would alert the local police who would in turn send round a car with suitably burly members of the Constabulary. Mrs Robinson, living on her own as she did, was quite taken with the idea of burly Constables. Charlie, detecting an interest, warmed to the task. He realised that the system was not cheap but he was sure that he could arrange a 20% discount if she agreed to a complete inventory of her household effects valued by a reputable insurance agency. She might find it hard to believe but people occasionally made claims that weren't strictly accurate and the insurance company through whom he dealt liked to know where it stood in such matters. In fact, he was so confident in the MSS (PP) that he had installed it himself. Perhaps she might like to come round and see how it worked?

As they left the house, Mrs Robinson asked rather coyly if a piece of plastic could really open a door. Charlie smiled, as you would to a child, withdrew his calfskin wallet from his pocket and removed with what amounted to a flourish his American Express Gold Card. He gestured to her to close the door, which she did, listening as always for the reassuring plop of the bolt in the latch. Charlie inserted the card between door and jamb and within seconds the former swung open. Mrs Robinson blinked. With the air of a man who had produced the necessary rabbit, Charlie extended an arm to the silver-blue BMW that lay in the drive. After ushering her into the left-hand seat in the rear, he closed the door with sufficient purpose to indicate her complete security, yet without a level of force that would cause alarm. Seated in the front, he continued his explanation, turning quarter profile to enhance what the grammatically challenged would call his best side. Once they arrived, he explained, he would not deactivate the MMS (PP) but allow it to alert the local police station. Before there was time for the panda cars to be sent in pursuit, he would ring the station desk and explain that he was merely demonstrating the system and that they were to call off the dogs. If she liked, she could speak to the authorities herself and obtain their opinion of the efficacy of the system.

They duly arrived. Charlie extended his front door key from its personalised pouch and opened the door. Nothing, as far as she could tell, appeared to happen. He went to the phone and dialled or, to be more accurate, tapped. Contact was made. The rescue mission was cancelled and the phone handed over. Mrs

Robinson was assured by a voice that he was indeed the desk sergeant, that there was a high success rate with this particular intruder preventative measure and that if more people like herself were to show an interest in sensible methods of crime control, society would be a better place for right thinking people to live in. Charlie then invited her to inspect the deactivating device that was situated in a rather constricted area under the stairs. He tapped in the four-number code and commented on the coincidence that it must be very close to the year in which she had been born. Mrs Robinson blushed slightly, moved as much by the compliment as by the inevitable contact that was made when he closed the door of the cupboard to demonstrate the subtle design that concealed the fact that there was a door there at all. She thanked Charlie profusely for all the time and trouble that he had taken and said she would certainly consider the opportunity very carefully. However, her plans were a little uncertain as she might be moving (the house was so large for one person) but she would certainly let him know as soon as she had decided. She, of course, had his card. But wasn't he going to a lot of trouble? Charlie assured her that he was in the risk business and his business was in risks. In fact, he would go so far as to say that the only *real* satisfaction in life came from taking a risk, putting, as the poet said, 'all your winnings on one turn of pitch and toss'. Anyway, she must make up her mind in her own time but, if she decided to move and as a consequence had to sell any of the furniture, he had much admired the mahogany drop-leaf table that stood in the hall and he would be prepared to make her an offer. Indeed, he smiled, perhaps one you could scarcely refuse. The table was grotesque but the porcelain piece on the lounge mantelshelf certainly wasn't.

In due course a Mr Duckworth arrived, who explained that Mr Shearing had instructed his company to conduct a valuation on behalf of the Insurance Company who, in turn, had underwritten the security system that she was proposing to purchase from the Shearing Agency. She asked him in and he proceeded to ooze his way through the house, clipboard in hand, lifting vases and tapping in a most impressively authoritative manner concealed parts of cupboards and the like with the cap of his ballpoint pen. Eventually, he reached the sitting-room where Mrs

Robinson was reading what appeared, from its cover, to be a rather lurid paperback novel. Mr Duckworth apologised for the intrusion and continued his lifting and tapping. He was in the vicinity of the fireplace when she was distracted by a short, but nevertheless sharp intake of breath. She looked up. Mr Duckworth was holding the porcelain piece in his hand. Mrs Robinson lowered the book to her lap and raised her eyes. Mr Duckworth explained that for a moment he had thought that it was the genuine article. But as a copy it was very good, very good indeed. Of course, the nature of the subject had spawned a multiplicity of imitations, mostly only fit for the fairground, but this was good, worth £50 or more. Mr Duckworth finished his labours and offered the inventory for inspection with a hint of genuflection. It absurdly reminded her of her late husband's clumsy efforts at what he considered the most important and, by defi-nition, the ultimate moment of her life. She ran her eye down the list. Perhaps, given the cost of removal companies, being burgled wasn't that bad after all. In particular, she noticed:

Item	*Mahogany Table, Drop Leaf*	*£200*
Item	*Porceline Figurine (reproduction)*	*£50*

Of course, Mr Duckworth explained, if she were not to take up what he considered a most favourable offer from Shearing Protection, she would probably find that her effects (so many fine pieces) were somewhat under-insured. His own company specialised in giving an exclusive service to households of this nature, at very little extra cost. If she wished, he could always call back, without any obligation, of course.

In the late morning of that day all the parties concerned had a number of calls they had to make. Mr Duckworth confirmed that the figurine was indeed genuine and he would be prepared to buy it, no questions asked, for £7,000 or even £7,500 if he could tie up an immediate buyer. It was up to Charlie to get her to cough. Mrs Robinson went into town, called at her solicitors and followed, though it was a bit of a rush, the appropriate advice. Returning, she called at Belladonna to tell the assistant that she might well change her mind and could they save the dress for another twenty-four hours, then into the Oxfam shop where she remembered seeing something that might prove useful. As she never tired of explaining to her friends, too often people used these places as disposal points for unwanted impedimenta. So it was only right, if only to encourage their efforts, that you bought the occasional article from time to time. In the evening she rang Mr Shearing to thank him for all the efforts he had made on her behalf but she would most probably be moving to be near her sister who was rather older than she. However, if he was still interested in the table, or anything else that might prove awkward to transfer to Norfolk, she would be in all tomorrow. Charlie, given the nature of Duckworth's offer, needed to know where he stood. Would there be any chance of this evening? He might go up to £500 but he was sure she understood that he would need to look at the piece rather more carefully than he had at first. Of course she understood and this evening would be no trouble at all—perhaps 8.30?—and after replacing the receiver she went to the bedroom to change and make herself up with more care than usual. Yes, the dress in Belladonna was ridiculously expensive, but it *was* very nice.

Charlie arrived on time and, after a careful inspection, suggested four-fiftyish for the table might be about right. Mrs Robinson seemed a little disappointed and almost on the point of refusing when Charlie, as an apparent afterthought, appeared to remember the existence of the figurine. The china ornament. Where was it? In the lounge? She might recall his aunt collected such items. After his mother had died so unexpectedly, she had... His voice trailed off. Throw that in and we'll call it five hundred. Mrs Robinson commented how nice it was in this selfish day and age that there were still some of the younger generation who thought about those who had brought them up. Of course he could have the piece. It would probably have been broken in the move in any event, but he did realise, didn't he, that it was only a reproduction, although apparently quite a good one. Charlie assured her that he was fully aware of what he was doing and, although his aunt was an absolute dear, she was very shortsighted. Would it be all right if he paid cash? While Charlie was as adept as the next when it came to the cheque's in the post routine, he felt on such occasions as these that it was better not to leave pieces of paper around which might prove incriminating. He would send a man round in the morning for the table. However, he might as well take the figurine himself.

By coincidence, at precisely the same point in time, Charlie and Mrs Robinson were doing their sums.

Charlie was at a loss. Things had gone awry. The arithmetic should have been simple. Twenty pounds to Harry to collect the table. Offload same for two hundred, maybe two fifty. Incidentals, say thirty. Expenditure three fifty max. Income, if Duckworth lived up to his promise, seven, seven and a half. Profit, six and a bit minimum, maybe seven. Not bad for a day's work. Yet at a loss he was. He had gone out in the morning, concluded a bit of unfinished business most satisfactorily, returned home, removed the figurine from its place of concealment in the cupboard under the stairs and set it with the cloth still covering it, rather theatrically, in the centre of the coffee table in the lounge. Switching on the television, he had watched the racing from Haydock and waited for Mr Duckworth to appear. Mr Duckworth was in a hurry and was already counting the fifties as he came through the door.

Seven, Charlie. That's right, isn't it?

Seven and a half, if I remember a'right.

Duckworth counted off ten more and, preparing to leave, removed the cloth and picked up the piece. As he reached the door he stopped and turned to Charlie with the expression of someone listening to a child protesting that he had been nowhere near the jampot, when the evidence was smeared across his face.

Come on, Charlie. This isn't your style. Where is it?

Where's what?

The one I saw yesterday. Which banana boat do you think...?

That's it. You've got it in your hand.

Duckworth continued in child-address mode.

This, Charlie, is a fake. It is not even a good fake. It is probably too modest to consider itself a fake. It is the sort of thing you can buy in any junk shop for 50p. Now where is the original?

I'm telling you. It's in your hand.

Now that he looked closer, Charlie saw that it wasn't the one he had acquired the evening before. The colours were more garish for a start. Surely he would have noticed that when she handed it over?

No, it's not in my hand.

Duckworth smiled and, loosening his grip, allowed the Dresden Shepherdess manqué to fall on to the parquet floor and smash into several very small pieces.

Mrs Robinson's calculations were somewhat more

complex. There were moral as well as financial matters to consider. Technically, it was a clear case of Breaking and Entering. But she had only ensured that Mr Shearing had the right and proper gift for his shortsighted aunt and the plastic had caused very little actual damage. In any event, as a lady in public she was naturally wearing gloves. If he had paid over the odds for the table, it was a case, as her late husband would have said, of *caveat emptor*. Indeed, her late husband must take a degree of responsibility for any turpitude that might have arisen. The confidence that had been the cornerstone of his commercial success had also led to whispers of immortality and, after he had collapsed at the height of a tirade against the Government which was strangling free enterprise, it was discovered that he had not, at this point, made any provision for the ill-considered widow.

However, if the figurine were to fetch £20,000, or even £25,000, given its condition, as the nice young man from the Manchester branch of that famous London Auction House had explained, and she were to sell the matrimonial home and its not, as she now knew, thanks to Mr Duckworth, inconsiderable effects, she should be able to buy that modest apartment in Harrogate that she had seen spotlighted in the *Telegraph* Property Columns and still have a surplus which, if properly invested, should produce a satisfactory income. There was no doubt that prudence dictated that she should have refused Mr Shearing's offer and never have allowed the possibility of this opportunity slipping from her grasp. But there had been something in the conditional Kipling reference that had struck a chord and, just once in your life, you should go to the wire—wasn't that the expression? Just once, otherwise you'd never know. And there was also the other side of this particular coin. That horrible little china object had been a much lauded present from her late husband's dear mother. The insistence of the woman that it stood, as it were *in loco parentis*, in the centre of the mantelpiece in her living room, never to be moved yet always to be dusted, had secured for that Arcadian figure a loathing that it scarcely deserved. If all had been left to her, she would, in due course, having summoned up the courage, have consigned it with the utmost satisfaction to the dustbin.

And there was the equally satisfactory matter of the £500 (her glance fell on the glossy bag stretched

across the sofa). The charming young lady at Belladonna had said that the result was simply stunning
and, even if that were not strictly true, there was no
doubt that viewed from every angle, as it most certainly would have been, it could only have met with
her late husband's complete disapproval.

As for Mr Charles A St J, there had been a moment
but those business cards were so... terribly tacky.

*And they were judged every man according
to their works*

Revelation, ch 20, v 13

The Grammar School Master
or *Vitai Lampada*

Adam was a good teacher. Of that, if you accepted
the collective view of Her Majesty's Inspectors,
Over Anxious Parents and Assorted Dinner Ladies,
there was no question. And, in that he had the inter-
ests of the pupils at heart and worked longer hours
than the great majority of his colleagues, he, no doubt,
passed muster with most other interested parties. The
school he taught at was a selective Grammar School,
which had served the community in a variety of guises
for the best part of five hundred years. During this
passage of history its title had changed. The epithet
'Free' had been added and subtracted according to
social conscience and aspiration. There was even a
time, in the last century, when 'Modern' had become
attached, a prefix of anticipation to herald the white-
hot technological revolution that was reputed to be
on the very lip of the horizon. However, wiser coun-
sels prevailed and mature consideration saw the

ephemeral nature of science when placed against the
permanence of Classical Antiquity and the experiment of frog-bottling and metal-detection slunk back
into the fume-cupboard, not to be released for another hundred years. The town ignored all such re-
launches and it was always referred to as t' Grammar
School and the inmates as t' Grammar School Boys
and Masters respectively.

Of course, Adam understood the function of selective education. The Ruling Classes, though not
adept at the higher flights of imaginative thought, had
the nous to devise a system that would find others to
do their thinking for them in what was becoming an
increasingly complicated world. When they ran out
of bright chaps of the right type, they had no alternative but to trawl the lower orders. This apparent egali-
tarian gesture made them much loved and allowed
the uninterrupted pursuit of proper activities, such
as chasing small furry animals and odd shaped balls.
It was these games handed down by the Great Public Schools that Adam particularly despised. To him,
they seemed to have been contrived with a level of
complexity which, if left to children, would never
have existed. No doubt, if it left The Dumb founded,

that was all to the good in the great scheme of things.

So Adam set out to redress the balance. At every opportunity he preached a social philosophy that more than made up in rhetoric what it lacked in substance. When approached by well-meaning persons who tried to persuade him to contribute to some cause that would support the disadvantaged, he would in return attempt to sell them a spurious raffle ticket, the proceeds of which were to assist the continued production of germ and chemical weapons. As he explained, if you are going to save the Government unnecessary expense you may as well be even-handed and do it across the board. In his support of child-centred learning, he had the expected runs-in with the Senior Members of Staff who tried to inculcate the 'Grammar School Ethos' but in the beginning he ignored them and later ridiculed their attempts to get him 'to see reason and play the game'. And he continued in his aims, confident of the rightness of his opinions.

However, in addition to the tirade, he also had a tactical weapon. His subject was English and through this he could influence minds not already blunted by the cudgel of the Mortgage Repayment. His message centred around the significance of the individuality of the task. He would stand before his class, a new exercise book held aloft. This, he explained, is not what it appears. It is not the commonplace staple of paper covered in red cardboard that you have received before. In this book I will find you, because only you will write in this book, and you will write what you think, what you believe, what you know. It will be a privilege for me to be allowed to enter your book. As a visitor I will consider and respect your point of view and your opinions. If I offer mine, it is with respect and in the way of help, as a guest might suggest a way to unblock a sink or rid the garden of a pest that is attacking the roses. This school exercise book is unique as it does not set out to produce a content that is marked right with a tick or wrong with a bad-tempered cross. There is no 'right' answer, no QED. Here is an empty space that demands no preconditions, waiting for you.

Yet, as a teacher, he knew it was not enough to preach or cajole. He knew he had to catch their attention. He had to entertain, not playing the fool but as a conjuror pulling rabbits and silk handkerchiefs from the most unexpected of hats. His lesson had to

be a show, a firework display that held the eye and
concentrated the mind, yet informed, directed and
warned against future pitfalls. A favoured trick was
when he was explaining, for the first time, the im-
portance of contrast to create tension. He would position himself at the side of an unoccupied desk. At
first he would sit on it, moving the point of focus
from its accustomed position. Then, as the explanation continued, he would stand and lift and lower
the hinged lid of the desk, as if fanning its contents
into the room. He would explain that if you wrote a
story where dramatic action followed dramatic action without pause or contrast, the tension would
slowly but surely ooze away. The story must breathe.
Have its peaks and troughs. It must ebb before it can
flow. You must have silence before you have... At
this point the swinging lid was at the top of its arc
and he slammed it down with all the force that one
hand allowed. To give time for the effect to sink in,
he would walk slowly to the front of the room before
turning and facing the class. Faces, half amused by
the circus, half appalled by the violence, looked back
and suitably smiled.

It was a Sunday morning and Adam, as usual, was

sitting at his desk in his classroom, marking. In front of him stood a pile of exercise books belonging to 3B. He not only taught 3B English, but he was also their Form Master. 3B, despite its nomenclature, was a first-year form of thirty boys. Unlike 3A, where most of the occupants were products of the preparatory section attached to the school, 3B was composed of scholarship boys from working class backgrounds. They were unpolished but usually unknowingly clever. It was this group to which Adam gave the most attention. Here was the raw material which could change attitudes and opinion.

He divided the books into three piles: two large and one small. The latter contained the work of the most promising boys and he would save them for last. The routine was the same. He would open the lid of each pupil's desk so that they stood before him like so many dominoes waiting to be played. After he had marked a piece of work, he would add his comments, suggesting rather than demanding improvements, place the book in its owner's desk and close the lid. One down, twenty-nine to go! After the first baker's dozen, he would stop for a cigarette. After the second, for a coffee. He was especially careful in his scrutiny of the remaining four. Even these he arranged in a pecking order and today he had decided to leave David's to last. He never added a numerical mark. As he pointed out to the Senior Master, a mathematician who had been sent by the Head to upbraid him in this unorthodoxy, perhaps the school considered that the cos theta of *Hamlet* was equal to the square root of *Macbeth*? The row rumbled on but in the end Adam won and it was agreed that if he could produce a form order that would satisfy the parents, he could mark in his own fashion.

The piece that he was examining was entitled 'A Moment of Real Disappointment'. He had explained to 3B that when given a title it was essential to look carefully at the words. The important word was 'Moment' rather than 'Disappointment'. What they were being asked was to describe a particular moment, the second or so when the disappointment sank in. Of course, they would have to describe the events that led to that moment but everything must be geared to it. When it arrived, the reader must be affected, the tension must be released. He realised he was asking a lot from eleven-year-olds but he knew that some of them would grasp the gist and, as the years went by, slowly assimilate this and connected ideas. He also explained why the word 'Real' had been added. It wasn't to suggest magnitude. It meant that he wanted them to have something to say that they knew about, that sprang from their own experience. So, no Space Ships and Pirates, please!

He picked up the last book. A single lid flagged that the end was nigh. He thought about switching on the overhead light but decided against it.

A Moment of Real Disappointment
by David Smith

I was a bit worried that day when I went to my Primary School, called St John's. My Dad, though he had come home from Hospital was still told to stay in bed. If he didn't get better soon, he wouldn't be able to take me to see United next Saturday. This would be really disappointing. Although I enjoyed reading and numbers and was on the top table, my real thoughts were about playing football in the afternoon after school.

My Mum had made some really nice sandwiches which I ate while waiting for the boys from Prexton Prep to arrive. They were quite snobby and said we were ignorant and couldn't speak properly. But we didn't mind as long as we won. My Dad says just because you speak posh doesn't mean that you can play football. I thought that because you speak posh doesn't mean you can't play football but my big sister Deborah told me not to be "too big for my boots". I was going to say that being "too big for your boots" wasn't much help at football but Mum gave me one of those looks so I didn't.

Anyway, the boys from Prexton Prep arrived and they all had the same coloured shorts and socks as well as shirts. They were bright red and looked very smart and quite big as well. The match kicked off and our teacher, Mr Weston, was the referee. It was soon clear that the Prexton Prep boys were very good this year and that there would be a very ~~good~~ hard match.

It was a bit like the comic that Pete had lent me. The ball went from end to end. Each side in turn having the opportunity to score the vital goal. Then the moment happened. I had never scored before and if I am honest I have to admit that I was lucky to even be in the team because as Mrs Beswick says there was a shortage of boys in our year. So whatever Sarah Hopkins says, we were always up against it.

Then it happened. Pete kicked the ball towards their goalie. He made a good stop but the ball bounced from his hands and landed just in front of me. The goal was there, empty. I couldn't miss. I kicked the ball. Oh no! I had missed but it hit the right side of the post and slowly bounced over the line. I had scored. Mr Weston blew the whistle at once. The game was over. We had won. All my team slapped me on the back. Even those who said I was a swot and sucked up to the teachers. The Prexton Prep boys just trooped off heads bowed. Their master looked very angry.

I couldn't wait to get changed and get home to tell Dad. I'd tell Mum, of course, but she wouldn't understand and just say "That's very nice, David". But Dad would understand. He used to tell me about the time when he played football himself and when he was better we would go to the Park and he would play in goal while I had shots in. He told me that if I practiced alot I would get better and I had to listen to what the teacher told me.

When I got back home I rushed into the hall, threw my kit on the floor, prepared to ignoer our Debbie's sarky remarks about messy boys and ran upstairs. Mum was standing at the top looking funny. The light from the landing window fell criss-crossed across her. Its O.K. Mum I'll put my bag away after. I just want to see Dad. I scored the winning goal. I whispered the last bit so that he shouldn't hear yet.

I could see now that Mum was not angry. I stopped on the stairs. She walked down as far as me sat on a step and sat me on her knee. I'm afraid I've got some terrible news, David. I'm afraid Daddy is dead. He died this afternoon.

So I couldn't tell him about the winning goal

and that was my moment of real disappointment.

Adam put down the superfluous pen, closed the book and, getting up in the manner of an old man, walked towards the last remaining desk. He placed the book carefully on top of its neatly piled fellows and looked over the desktop into the fading light, before closing the lid without any perceptible sound.

A Man Who Was Lost For Words

Y ou were trying hard to justify your decision. You had, when all was said and done, waited a long time. The appointment was for 9.30 and it was gone ten when you had left. The heat in the waiting-room had become increasingly oppressive. That child would not stop crying and the fits and starts of coughing and sneezing had begun to convince you that the visit would do more harm than good. And, anyway, there had been no repetition of that funny turn. So, reassured, you walked through the market place to Al's Cafeteria. Nevertheless, although looked at from all sides the logic was irrefutable, there was still the dark shadow of ill-ease. It wasn't the doctor's fault that the appointments were running late. No doubt he had had someone like that dreadful Harrison woman holding him up for half an hour. There was nothing wrong with her, just a chance to moan and pick up bits of gossip: 'I see that Mr So-and-So is in the waiting room. I do hope it's nothing serious.' It was, moreover, the second time you had failed to attend. The first time you had forgotten or, if not exactly forgotten, allowed the event to slip your memory. And, at the deepest and darkest point in that crease of uncertainty, was a curiosity or at least a need to discover why you had passed out on that particular day. It had been something of a shock to come round on the Fulton Circular at 8.30 in the dark, when you knew that you had boarded the double-decker just after lunch to make the short journey into town. In future, you wouldn't go upstairs. Had people assumed that you were asleep–or worse? At bottom, that was what was most mortifying. To be classed with the toe-rags that picked up their Tesco's Breakfasts in luridly emblazoned cans. Still, to be unaware for eight hours was disturbing. And there was the little matter of the blurred vision and the occasional pain in the chest.

So there you were, sitting at your favourite table on Al's ground floor. You were probably scanning the newspaper for headlines when you heard the conversation of two elderly and overweight women who, in a series of slaloms, were descending the stairs.

The gist of the discussion was whether shopping at Sainsbury's was betraying their class. They crossed the floor of the café before negotiating the final obstacle that barred their exit through the shop and into the street.

Mind the step!

What?

Watch the step. Didn't you see it? There's a notice that says WATCH THE STEP.

As usual, your mind reacted and started the game. Did you mind the step as you mind the baby? For how long were you expected to watch the step? Would someone ring a bell when the watch was over? Would there be a dog watch? Was there a dog to watch? Although you would never have admitted it, you took a real pleasure in playing with words. A Wordsmith, as Grandad was a Blacksmith. A Worker with Words. A Keeper of Words. That was the reason for the headline business. Of course, some were better than others. The typographical error was noted but not applauded; 'Cod Biting off East Coast of Scotland' was satisfactory if not memorable, but these had to be taken on board for the moment of the real gems.

GOLFER SCORES HOLE IN ONE
WITH SHOT OFF SPECTATOR'S LEG

was a particular favourite. It had started off as a private game but by now, you had to admit, it had become a little bit obsessive.

When you found a suitable example, you copied it into a notebook which you carried for that purpose and, on reaching home that evening, you would meticulously enter the product of the day's travail into a series of ledgers. These were divided by 'Method': Pun, Innuendo, Ambiguity (accidental), Ambiguity (intentional), Spoonerism, Malapropism and the like—terms that had been found in your well-thumbed Fowler's *English Usage*—and cross-referenced by 'Subject': Politics, Domestic, Sport, Medicine and so on.

The turning point, if there was a turning point—perhaps it would be better described as a steepening of the slope, anyway, a particular moment—was the Tractor Headline. Not that that had any value in the grand scale of things but the phrasing directed you to the article below. Unusually, you read it. It didn't make sense at first. A farmhand driving a tractor had occasion to traverse an unmanned railway crossing.

As a warning there was a notice:

DO NOT CROSS
WHILE RED LIGHT IS FLASHING.

The labourer waited until the light turned to red, then drove his tractor, the trailer and himself under the Euston Express. Then you realised. It was a recalled phrase from childhood that stirred the memory: 'I won't see you while Friday, Walt.' Some shibboleth that floated, once a week, on the night air after Father and friend paused for a moment on their return from The Rose and Crown. But there again, it wouldn't have happened to Father; he always boasted that he couldn't read or write. Perhaps Mother's views on the advantages of an education were wrong after all.

If this tossed the first pebble of doubt into the pool of your complacency, the Radio Programme threw the whole affair into jacuzzi mode. (You liked the wireless in equal proportion to the way you hated the Television. Better pictures, for a start and the other was also a 'T' word. Television, Telephones, Talking at breakfast—a trinity to be avoided at all cost. It was a letter invented to annoy, with its patronising tut and its adjectival posturing.) The programme had been about words and how they were abused for propaganda purposes. It was, it seemed, the chief weapon of the dictator, who could use them to enter your mind and reprogramme your understanding. This was particularly true of the English language which, with its ambiguities, was often open to more than one meaning. The presenter started with a lighthearted example which caught your attention as it fell into your own sphere of research:

DOGS MUST BE CARRIED

ON THE ESCALATOR.

OFFENDERS WILL BE PROSECUTED.

The purpose of this notice was clearly to avoid unnecessary accident to either human or animal and could only cause confusion to the perverse. However, he explained that in a totalitarian state it, or something like it, could take on a more sinister meaning. There was a time when you would have been privately amused at the thought of some official standing at the foot of the stairs, offering Chihuahuas for the frail, Great Danes for the macho and Poodles for the fashion conscious, but now your mind drifted in a different direction. The programme continued with references to Orwell and Kafka but you had stopped

listening and, without realising, pressed the off button. The more you thought about it, the more you
felt the momentary loss of control that is experienced
when you step up a stair that isn't there. Ever since
they had moved you here, you had received notices
and reminders to go here, go there. Perhaps it was
part of some elaborate experiment. Perhaps you had
not understood what was really meant by 'This is for
your own good.' One of those brown envelopes had
arrived that morning. You hadn't opened it (in fact,
it was still lying on the mat under the letterbox) but it
was clearly official. The window that covered the
typed name and address could only mean another
instruction disguised as a polite request. During your
meanderings between home and café you turned the
problem over in your mind. Headlines lost their ap-
peal and more and more time was spent at home
with your second enthusiasm, the measuring of your
own vocabulary. This was done by counting in the
dictionary the words of which you knew the meaning. You had started at *aardvark* (which you did know)
and would finish at *zymurgy* (which you wouldn't).
You were scrupulously honest. Only one word per
stem and no compounds were allowed. Nor were half

understood words, *disinterested* and the like. As a final act, you would choose one word from each column that was entirely unknown and, printing them out in large letters on small pieces of card that you kept for that purpose, pin them on to a cork board in the kitchen.

The mail continued to flop through the letterbox and was studiously ignored. The list of words grew through grim determination. The more you understood, the less you could be confused. The cards were transferred from the board to a drawer, where they were systematically graded and regraded as UN-SAFE, SAFE and VERY SAFE. Once the door bell rang insistently but, by taking a firm grip of the edge of the table, you resisted the temptation to answer it. You were coming down the stairs one day when you saw through the landing window with its criss-crossed mock lead panes a man in a suit, carrying a briefcase, walking up the garden path. Stand completely still. The doorbell rang twice. You heard the clap of the letterbox and before long the man returned into view and left. Another brown envelope. It was then that you decided. You couldn't afford to be in the house during the day. Nor the café either. The best plan was to leave the house by the back door at first light and not return until darkness fell. They would be too busy in the pub or whatever they did to bother you then. Slowly the plan took shape. To go back to your beginnings, to rediscover the woods, fields and streams that you had half remembered, half forgotten from those other days. You unplugged the wireless, wrapped the flex around the casing and put it on the top shelf of a cupboard. You were now as safe as you could be.

So, the next and subsequent mornings, you got up, made the bed and, while eating breakfast, prepared your supper. You put the contents of the bowl into a slow cooker and switched it on. It would be ready on your return. Although the area you lived in was built up for some distance in all directions, it was not difficult to escape undetected. You left by the back way and reached in a few yards a bridge that crossed the canal. Once the towpath was joined, a walk of half an hour or so led out of the suburbs and past the upmarket residential area of Stockworth. It would be even shorter if the lengthy meander were missed by cutting a corner through a scrap-dealer's yard. You had tried it once, only to be confronted by an alsatian-cross that tore out of its kennel and leapt in the direction of your face. Fortunately its ambition was stopped in mid-air by the rope attached to its neck. But the rope was already frayed and, anyway, if you followed the canal you could always watch the waterhens that nested on the bend.

Once past the big houses whose gardens were buttressed by pasture, you stepped out into the open countryside. Field paths and disused sunken lanes led pleasantly through the cultivated land to the edge of the moor. The dishevelled appearance of rock and heather reinforced the memories of unfettered childhood, a sharp contrast to the regimentation of recent days. However, the sense of temporary release was always checked when you reached the point where the land began to swell before it broke as the steep gritstone escarpment of Wild Boar Edge. This was the boundary of the grouse moor owned by Mr Michael Myte, CBE, a local worthy in a number of senses of the word, who had made his money by persuading people to buy things they didn't really need and his reputation by giving a tithe to the Tory Party. The whole area, some 5,000 acres, was barbed-wired and where gates broke this stalag uniformity, they were emblazoned with a far from ambiguous notice:

DANGER
HIGH VELOCITY RIFLES
IN CONSTANT USE.

It was also heavily keepered.

One advantage of starting early was that you were usually past this section before others were about. Nevertheless, you had discovered a breach in the defences, where a stream and a variety of animals, unaware of the sanctity of land ownership, had opened up a gap. Using the undulating ground as cover, it was easy enough to cross the mile or so of 'Grouse & Rough Shooting Rights' and, by way of a rocky gully that split the cliff face, reach the Right of Way that ran along the top of the Edge. To reach the top was always a moment of quiet pleasure. The uneasy mixture of fear of detection and muscular fatigue was fanned into a sense of relaxed content-ment by the draught of air that always stirred, no matter how calm the valley. You would sit on a rock, suck a boiled sweet, give the eyes a chance to settle and watch, waiting for the hen harriers. Although unu-sually south, there was no doubt that this was their territory. They would quarter the area, plunging and swooping in their search for food. The larger female was by far the more active. The male, slate grey, as often as not followed her to the kill. Too idle to work for himself.

Once on the Edge, there was unrestricted access and, depending on mood and weather, you would either keep to the high ground or slip into the limestone valleys that lay within the horseshoe of grit. Only Thursday demanded a routine. Then your journey followed a stream or, at first, a trickle, fed by drops of rain that slid down that particular side of the watershed, eventually to flow via the Trent into the North Sea. After a couple of miles it was joined by another and, just below this confluence, was crossed by a packhorse bridge at a point known as Three Counties Meet. In previous times it had been the rendezvous for a variety of rogues who, on the approach of the Constabulary of one County, could escape, in a matter of moments, into the immunity of another. The fall of your feet echoed those of previous generations who had also avoided detection by leaving your county of residence and descending into a small town where you were unknown. Having drawn your weekly emolument (a recent addition) from the Post Office, you'd buy your provisions and, slinging the canvas hold-all across your back, return the way you came. If the weather was really bad or if you felt more tired than usual, you would treat yourself to a mug of hot, sweet tea and catch the bus that circumnavigated the high ground. Of course, you would get off at the outskirts, regain the canal and time the whole affair to arrive home in the dark. You didn't often take the bus. It was expensive and there was always the danger you might miss the stop.

On this particular Thursday, you woke with a sense of gloom. Perhaps it was the pain in the chest that seemed over the last few days to have become more insistent, perhaps it was the arrival of another brown envelope, perhaps it was just annoyance at forgetting the mixed herbs for the stew that was to simmer in the slow cooker, ready for your return. Anyway, you left the house in a bad mood and a hurry. Your annoyance was not sufficient to brave the alsatian but, by the time you reached the property of the aspirant knight, you eschewed (ditto) your usual route and strode defiantly along the skyline. This took you to a different point on the Edge but a grassy rake promised an easy ascent to the top. It was during this approach that you became aware of the female harrier, clearly in some distress, sweeping along the face of the cliff before gliding out into the moor to perch on a fence post. After a few moments the performance was repeated. The foot of the rake revealed the reason. A dead rabbit, its skin slit by a knife to reveal the by now ravaged flesh, lay unnaturally exposed on a ledge. A few yards higher lay the male raptor, still-eyed. You returned to the rabbit and, moving it some yards from the original site, piled rocks above and around it in such a way that it could do no further damage. Was there any point in doing anything else? The female was back at her post, waiting for the man to move. You turned up your collar, thrust your hands in your pockets and at an unnecessarily rapid pace strode to the rim.

You continued along the Edge in the direction of the Three Counties bridge. Half way along there was an undercut promontory which jutted out towards the moor and the converted farmhouse owned by the Mighty Myte. If you walked to the end of the salient, you finished some way from the cliff itself, balanced, as it were, in space. You stood on the very lip and looked in bitter anger at the house below. A Range Rover turned into the drive, spilling a group of children on to the gravel. You watched the little specks dashing aimlessly hither and thither until a woman got out of the driver's side and shepherded them towards the front door. If they had looked up, they might have seen a silhouette perched on the edge of all things, tugging the collar of the grey trench coat tighter around its neck as your lids fell, partially hooding your eyes against the wind.

It was as you were crossing the bridge that you realised that you had forgotten your Post Office Book. The whole thing was a waste of time. They would never give you any money without the book. Even if you pretended that you had lost it, they would require proof of identity. A further search of the pockets and bag drew a blank on both accounts. You had that feeling again, the feeling of panic, as though there was something inside you that had taken over control. Better not to go back over the moor. Better to drop, however fruitlessly, into the town and get the bus home. There was just enough money left from last week for the fare. Although the bridleway was neither steep nor rough, you stumbled more than once before the track turned into tarmac. You were beginning to feel very tired and finding it difficult to focus. You remembered that there was a bench outside The Fox and Grapes and it seemed reasonable to sit on it for a few moments to collect yourself. Perhaps have a little sleep. Not for long. Just till the bus came.

There were only two further matters to report. The first was when Dave Smith and his wife left The Fox and Grapes at closing time and virtually tripped over the legs that sprawled from the bench on to the pavement. Although Dave was of the certain opinion that the man was drunk, he allowed his wife's more compassionate explanation, that he was ill, to prevail and returned to the bar to phone an ambulance. When medical help arrived, it was found that he was neither drunk nor ill and the subsequent post-mortem merely added confusion to an already confusing affair. Doctors were at a loss to understand why the symptoms, which must have been apparent, had not been diagnosed and acted upon. It was not as though the man was a tramp.

The second happened in another County and reached for different reasons a similar vacuum of indeterminacy. In the end, Mrs Harrison had made the decision. She was not a busybody but she knew she had a duty as a neighbour. The curtains had not opened or closed for at least eight days and her knocks on the door had produced no response. Making sure that no one was about, she pushed up the flap of the letterbox and peered into the hall, which was only intermittently lit by the light that filtered through an upstairs window. She turned her head so that she could listen more carefully and, hearing nothing, arched her neck so that she could examine the hall carpet. The area close to the door seemed to be covered with what appeared to be a pile of rubbish, but as her eyes became accustomed to the gloom, she started to distinguish individual shapes that eventually focused into envelopes and slim plastic-covered parcels. If he hadn't picked up his mail...

She lifted the receiver and dialled 999. For some reason she remembered how, years ago, she had been taught to do this in the dark or a smoke-filled room. Place a finger in each of the last two holes on the dial...

Hello. Yes, hello. Yes. Police, please.

Perhaps that was a mistake. Perhaps an ambulance was more important, or even the Fire Brigade to break in.

Yes, hello. It's my neighbour. I haven't seen him for...

Sorry, yes. Harrison. Nellie -Helen- Harrison. My neighbour at number 42...

Yes, I live at 40, Riverdale Avenue. Could you come round? I'm sure something's wrong.

Yes. Thank you. Yes, I will. I will. Thank you.

She hung up and, moving to the wall next to the window, leant on it in such a way that she could see next door's gate without being seen herself. It took longer than she had imagined for the police car to arrive and two policemen to get out. The older checked the numbers on the semis and, opening the gate, walked up the path to her front door. The younger, for no apparent reason, returned to the driver's side and appeared to check something on the steering column. Once satisfied, he proceeded up the parallel path and started to peer through the windows. After Mrs Harrison had been reassured that she had taken the right action, the two joined forces at the front door.

Well, son, can you smell gas?

Sarge?

Gas. Wouldn't you say that you can smell gas?

Oh, yes, Sarge. Gas. Definitely gas.

Well, don't just stand there. Break a window and effect an entry.

The constable did as he was told. Broke a small window that ran vertically along the side of the door, slipped the safety chain and placed a rather stiff Yale lock on the sneck.

Come on, lad. It can't be that hard. You have sorted all the locks, I suppose?

It's not locked, Sarge. It's sort of jammed.

With a final effort, the Guaranteed Prize Winning Offer from *The Readers' Digest* was unjammed and the inspection began. The constable soon returned from the first floor.

Nothing much there. Bed's made. The place is neat and tidy, except for the wardrobe which is full of empty Coke bottles. Perhaps he's gone on holiday.

The sergeant was in the kitchen, looking at the table that had been set for a meal. He had just taken a boiled sweet out of a large jar that stood on a work surface and was starting to unwrap it when he heard the sound of a slight click. He lifted the lid of the slow cooker. What appeared to be some sort of stew started to re-bubble, in response to the thermostat, for what must have been the umpteenth time.

No, I don't think that he decided to go on holiday, son. It's my guess that this was his supper.

The Loitering Heirs

I*t was the best of times.*

The older of the two men standing at the bar paused in mid-sentence and nodded nostalgically.

Yes, it was the best of times. The Estate Agent sold the property; the Mortgagee put up the cash; the Lawyer held the monies and paid out the dividend. The caretaker safeguarded the property, kept the structure up to scratch and enhanced the herbaceous border. What is more, he did this out of his own pocket, serviced the loan and subsidised the local council. In due course, the caretaker's wife would suggest that they might move on in the world. Whereupon the first gallant gentleman would revalue the property and he, the money lender and the holder of forensic mysteries would again dip their hands in the pot and draw out their just reward.

The younger of the two, who had been listening attentively, was about to interject when Roger continued:

Of course, in those days we had a Government that knew the meaning of the word. Led by a man of vision. He had no truck for the Looney Left, Parlour Pinks or Johnny Foreigner. Straight to the heart of the matter. If in doubt, blow 'em out of the water. CREATE WEALTH FOR ONE AND YOU CREATE WEALTH FOR ALL. That was the watchword and I am proud to say that we did not shirk our responsibility in the matter. When we deemed the time propitious, we added a further zero to the value, or price, as the case might be, and everyone got wealthier and wealthier. There was even a time when the caretakers made a couple of bob out of it. Yes, you could say it was the best of times. Life was simple, straightforward and, above all, David, clean.

David was young enough to consider this evaluation a trifle cynical but Roger's reputation in the commercial world stepped out before him and who was he, a mere beginner, to contradict the Candymaster, a man who could tempt the innocent into willingly entering upon situations that, inevitably, disintegrated to his advantage?

No, it's not so easy now. But there are ways. There are ways. Take repossession, for example. Possession might be nine-tenths of the law, but repossession is the 10% gilt-

edged certainty. Repos usually go to auction and the astute bidder can get a bargain. By definition, the property looks down-at-heel—if you can't afford the mortgage, you certainly don't splash out on paint and bedding plants—and this, with a few judicious enquiries from my goodself about sup-posed rights of way or putative planning applications for change of use to neighbouring properties, will deter the faint-hearted. The Mortgagee is usually keen to get what he can and try to chase the balance through the Courts. Buy at knock-down prices—tart it up—sort out short-term lets with ICI for their itinerant employees—and wait for the market to recover. The only legwork is being in the right place at the right time. It's a matter of keeping your ear to the ground. You are in the business, David. You catch my drift?

David, though young, had caught the drift.

What are you on a year, David? I should guess... He mentioned a figure that was flatteringly in excess of reality.

But there's always room for a little more. Information is a commodity and like any commodity...

David nodded and accepted the proffered card with its embossed legend of Corley Associates, Commercial and Property Consultants.

Have another drink, old chap. As you are new in town,

I'll tell you what, I'll take you down to the Cricket Club. You'll meet all sorts of useful people down there and, for some reason, plenty of women. Do you play yourself?

David shook his head.

Pity. It helps if you have an understanding of the game. No point in chatting up the wife of some rabbit that's going to be out first ball. In my experience, numbers three or four in the order are usually the best bet for a lengthy innings. If he's out in the middle, he can't be behind the pavilion, if you follow my logic. You must come down, David. Fine game, cricket. You can't beat the soft smack of willow on leather or whatever the lady's wearing.

   ...

I'm more of a soccer man myself.

The back of the chair she sat in caught the remnants of a weak November sun and the reflected light exposed, rather cruelly, the slight scrawniness that was beginning to show on her neck, an ageing process that had been accelerated as much by worry as by time. Where had she gone wrong? After all, she had done much to put it right. Or so she had thought. She had quickly realised that the key was to avoid the circumstances of her parents. Mother subordinate to a Father who drank. Living in a terrace house outflanked by an outside toilet with cut up sheets of the *Daily Mirror* (I'll have no truck with no flaming Tory rag) harpooned on a rusting nail. As a child, waiting in fear for the clash of the back gate and the accusations over nothing, punctuated only by dumb silences. Even at that age she knew that the route of escape was into a middle class with its semi in the suburbs and the company car parked in the drive. After that, who knows?

A bitter blow had been delivered on her fifteenth birthday. Father had returned earlier than usual to announce that she no longer had to go to school. He had spoken to that Miss Williamson who had some high-falutin idea that his daughter might take O Levels and go to college (with the rest of the Tory flamers) but he had soon put *her* right. A girl's place is in a mill until she's married, then it's in the kitchen. University! That's what's wrong with this country. Women getting above their station. The thought of losing the vision that Miss Wilkinson had uncased caused her for the first time to resist. But, with no ally, it was not long before she was sitting on the production line with a mouth that was still sore and slightly swollen. It was at this point that she realised that dumb acceptance was, after all, a form of subterfuge and set out to sort matters herself. Without anyone knowing, she went to night-school, where her faith in equal opportunity was rekindled by a young teacher from the local Grammar School. Perhaps it was him, or perhaps just her, but the fact was that she passed every exam with ease and in a very short time was able to leave the mill and join a local Estate Agent. Here, it quickly became apparent that, despite his unwillingness to accept it, she was more intelligent than her immediate boss. So, it was to his credit that he explained how she could move on. To his debit that he assumed a quid pro quo. But she was growing worldly-wise by the week and, with no real difficulty, fended off his advances whilst accepting those of a major Insurance Company in Manchester.

It was about this time that Mother died and Father panicked. Still, blood is blood and she had stayed at home. Slowly the ground rules changed. His excuses for avoiding work and joining his cronies at the Stew grew thinner and the day when he asked her for the loan of a few bob until Friday was the day the façade caved in. He, of course, had not changed. But his self-assertion had drooped and he spent the time moaning, to those who would listen, about changing values and how things were not as they were. By and large, he kept out of her way. The deal was that she ironed his shirts and he left her alone.

Eventually, her combined skills led to domestic dominance and further steps up the promotional ladder. It was at this point that she met Tom. He was on his way up. She could see that. Schoolteachers and estate agents were all very well, but Tom had ambition and ideas. She didn't set out to 'get' Tom but she opened the gate and it was not long before she had accepted an invitation from his parents to come round for dinner. She liked them. They were comfortably off and put their energies into good works and long walks. As a result, her main preoccupation was the presence of Father in the equation. If he should come out of the woodwork. But Fate was kind and the dilemma was resolved. Father returned home from the pub more embittered than usual. He visited the outside toilet and in a fit of pique pulled the chain with such violence that the cistern flew off the wall and, hitting him on the head, killed him. It was reported in the Stew, but not in the local paper, that the section of the *Daily Mirror* that he had clutched in his hand bore the challenging headline:

TORIES WORKING AT OWN CONVENIENCE?

So, she was able to leave Stanley Street (formerly known as Dog Lane) and set up a 'room of her own' near her place of work. The fact that she had to rent, as the Building Society were wary of potentially pregnable women, only confirmed her views. In contrast, the affair with Tom progressed famously. The marriage duly took place amongst the usual plethora of cut glass and approving smiles. They bought a cottage by the river which was clearly too small but nevertheless irresistible. The final corner had been turned and the road ahead seemed straight and forward. Tom soon reached the Board and his acumen invited a variety of directorships. Wisely, he saw that his talents were producing rewards for others rather than themselves. He set up his own business, which flourished, and it was not long before they contemplated a move to Stockworth. In her estate agent days, even the bosses had talked about Stockworth with a certain reverential awe, so when Tom suggested that they had a look at a property on, of all places, The Lawns, she knew that, no matter how the metaphor was mixed, her boat had come in.

So, where had she, they, gone wrong? It was too easy to blame the recession and the false dawn of her father's flaming Tories. She knew where the reality lay. It was the dinner parties, expensive holidays and her insistence that the children had to be privately educated that had eaten up the equity on which, if the truth were told, they had always relied. They had made so much on the cottage. Was it wrong to suppose that it wouldn't happen again? It certainly wasn't Tom's fault. He had tried to spread the net. He had been encouraged to borrow short-term against the house. He got up earlier and earlier and arrived home later. It had reached the situation where life consisted of little more than work and sleep. Or rather, in her case, not sleeping, as Tom had taken to mumbling to himself during the night. This would first wake and then drive her out of bed. She would sit at the nursery window looking over the fields to the canal. Each morning, she would wait for that solitary figure who appeared walking along the towpath soon after first light, measuring his bowed head and hands slouched in overcoat pockets against her own abjectness, then go down to the kitchen and make herself a cup of coffee lined with a large brandy. And, of course, that stupid business at the Cricket Club had not helped, even if Tom had never found out.

She heard the crunch of footsteps on the gravelled drive. Naturally, the car had been one of the first things to go. She knew that Tom had been to see if he could do anything about the repossession. She turned on a lamp and looked into the mirror to tidy her hair. Her mother looked miserably back. Tom entered the lounge but she knew the outcome before he, almost apologetically, shook his head. The light through the window had virtually gone but she could detect something frighteningly familiar in the figure silhouetted against it with its bent head and drooping shoulders.

I have a Mr Lenehan on the line. Will you take the call?

Lenehan? Lenehan. Oh yes, put him through. David! How nice to hear from you. You have? Excellent. Hang on a sec. I'll get a pen. Right. Fire away. 3, The Lawns,

Stockworth. Nice area. Is there a reserve fixed? Really. That's low. Times must be hard. Excellent. Look, I'll tell you what I'll do. You pop into the pub after work and I'll let you know how we've got on.

David wasn't happy with the arrangement but he needed the money. Yet, during the remainder of the afternoon, he managed to convince himself it wasn't his fault that people bought beyond their means and, after all, Head Office had approved his valuation of the reserve. Having cheered himself up, he started to calculate the potential mark-up. Ten per cent of that would be a useful sum. It would certainly sort his current problem. He began to feel more relaxed. Not bad for the price of a phone call. Of course, Roger would have to deliver. No problem. Roger would deliver. He wasn't called the Candymaster for nothing.

It was starting to get dark as he approached the pub. He looked in the carpark to see if Roger had arrived but there was no sign of the Jag. He went into the bar and ordered a large orange, which he drank in one go. It seemed a bit weak. Perhaps the barman had only put one in. He reordered and watched carefully. The barman went to the vodka optic. The pump rose and fell and the orange, already opened, was quickly added.

I said a large orange, chum. Same as last time.

I'm sorry, sir. I thought you said a single. I don't know why they have the music on so loud.

Come on, Roger. Where are you? He didn't like this place and could never understand why Roger insisted they met there. The music was too loud and, as a consequence, people shouted rather than talked. A group that appeared to be arguing over a rabbit was particularly getting on his nerves. Perhaps a cigarette would help. Where on earth was his lighter? He was sure he had left it with the packet on the bar. That bloke's got one. I'll ask him. Thanks, pal. The drink was starting to get to him and his irritation increased. Why wouldn't that fool simply accept that Cyril, whoever he was, had not been in? Come on, Roger! The front door opened. Half a Lager Joe. That's all we need.

At half past eight, Roger arrived and started to steer his way through the crowds that only crept out of the woodwork at Christmas.

What'll you have, Sharon?

I dunno. What are you having?

I dunno.

Whoever gave women the vote? David lifted his glass to indicate his presence and looked to see if he could gauge Roger's mood. It didn't appear promising. A dark brooding seemed to seep from a furrowed brow. Eventually, he reached the bar and inserted an elbow between David and Sharon's bacardi and coke.

So sorry! Haven't I seen you at the Cricket Club? Bailey's over ice. Good choice. No, just the usual orange.

David tried to control his impatience. Roger had by this time eased himself into pole position. His right hand in a position to offer a light to Sharon's more attractive friend. His left, fist lightly clenched, was resting on the bar between himself and his accomplice.

Well! Did it go or not?

Roger, still with his back half towards David, rolled over his left hand and, with a theatrical gesture, opened it slowly. A gold-coloured key shone in his palm.

They Still Stop For Ambulances–
Don't They?

As the train approached the station which he had not visited for thirty years, the now not so young man sat a little uneasily. Whether this was caused by the ill-fitting suit they had assigned him or whether he was apprehensive about his return to his home town, unaccompanied, he was not sure. But, as the train pulled into the station, he sat with expectation on the edge of his seat, peering out of a window that was blurred by a mixture of drizzle and dust. It wouldn't take him long to get off. He had only a small hand bag which was tucked safely between his feet.

However, the portion of the train to which he had been firmly directed did not stop at a platform but on a bridge outside. There was a surge of panic. Perhaps he should have been in the forward section. Perhaps he should try to move along, but he remembered that an earlier investigation to find a lavatory had been met by a sealed door. The train restarted.

What was the next stop? Would they allow him to use his transit-warrant to come back? Would he arrive too late—when it was all over? The train stopped once more. He was now by the automatic doors and, to his relief, the blue light flashed and the portions separated and folded back. He was home.

As soon as he alighted, he heard the instruction over the Tannoy. The tone of the voice, whilst not threatening, had a suggested menace:

All transit persons must board the moving walkway. Do not attempt to move forward. Do not jostle.

Not, at this time of day, that there was much chance of jostling. His fellow travellers consisted of a frail old woman carrying a plastic shopping bag and a tattooed youth whose bandaged arm was a poor attempt to disguise the electronic tag. He was in the process of wondering what had happened to the others, the smartly dressed group that had emerged from the VIP lounge just before the train left Euston, when he caught a glimpse of the last of them, side by side, laughing and talking, being transported along a different plastic tube towards what appeared to be the station concourse. In contrast, the track that he was on was constructed in such a way that the passengers would be forced first into single file and then on to individual moving pads. Again the Tannoy:

Each transit-person must occupy a single pad. In the event of a breach of instructions, the walkway will cease to operate. An immediate fine will be imposed on any offender. Inability to pay will lead to confiscation of goods.

He placed his feet carefully in the middle of the pad and clutched his bag close to his body. He reached a glass partition, which opened and closed behind him. The pad stopped and he realised that he was encased in a small area by a further partition that separated him from the old woman. After she had passed out of sight, the partition opened and the pad carried him out, not on to the concourse, but into the street itself.

Although this was much the same, it had an unfamiliar air. The café was still there, no longer Pete's Eats but, according to the flashing neon, KWIK-SNAX. The pet shop had gone, as had the ironmongers. He noticed the bookshop had been converted into a video-hire. He was sorry about that. Not that he read much but, as a man who had worked with his hands, he recognised the trouble that was taken to produce good quality goods and he recalled the care that potential purchasers used when they opened and inspected the contents, cupping the palms so as not to strain the spine. Also, it had been run by a most elegant lady. Then, an inward smile–anyway, the King Bill was still there. He would know a face or two in there, at least. Of course, Charlie would have moved on, he always had an eye for the main chance, but maybe he'd find Big H and Ant or Billy, or even that bloke who was a schoolteacher or something, who seemed to know a lot but didn't know anything really–more holidays than the Queen–that was the crack. Anyway, there would be someone who would tell him what he wanted to know.

Seeing the road was clear of traffic, he stepped off the kerb to cut diagonally across the street. No sooner had his foot landed on a strip of yellow plastic paint, which he had supposed indicated a restriction on parking, than a klaxon shrieked and he was again aware of the voice that he had heard in the station:

You have stepped into a restricted zone. Do not continue. Instead, proceed to the appropriate crossing. If unsure, report to the kiosk immediately to your left.

He looked in the indicated direction and saw the tattooed youth was already crossing at the policed intersection. The old lady was still painfully making her way towards the same point. He knew his exit-warrant would not safeguard him against the more serious misdemeanours. So, feeling it wise to follow the instructions, he set off to follow the woman. She was moving so laboriously that he was sure to over-take her at his present, slightly panicky pace, so he deliberately slowed that he might arrive at the kiosk immediately after her. It could be important to see what she did.

As they approached the crossing point, a young boy wearing clothing appropriate to the playing of an American fieldsport and gliding at speed on roller-blades appeared in the opposite direction. He had no intention of slowing and it was clear that the woman would have to get out of his way. Her eva-sive action was complicated by a reduction in width of the pavement by a large electrical junction box. He saw that she was in no-man's land, not sufficiently agile to turn back nor sufficiently active to accelerate forward. A collision seemed inevitable. As the boy approached (why wasn't he at school?) she turned sideways and clung to the top of the box. He was close enough to notice that she shut her eyes. An arm of the skater caught the carrier bag, splitting the fragile plastic and spilling the contents. The blades hissed past. The boy, with arrogant ease, spun to skate backwards for a few yards and gave his opinion of the event before disappearing:

Watch where you're going, scumbag! and—what appeared as a final telling insult—*Ped!*

He helped her pick up her groceries. Some badly bruised sprouts, a yellowing cauliflower and a tin of cat food. By this time she had tied the original open end of the bag together in a clumsy but effective knot and offered the split section as an aperture to refill the bag. Once the purchases were secured, she rolled the plastic together to form some sort of a grip and without a word continued up the street. Clearly, it had happened before. She reached the crossing place, showed a card and went across. The man in the kiosk glanced up and then continued to read his paper. He was not certain what his next move should be.

Is it all right if I cross here?

ID? He produced the exit warrant. The man looked first at it, then at him. His only expression was a slight scowl.

Make sure you've checked back before your personal curfew.

The laminated card was returned.

He stood at the edge of the kerb watching a red light and the traffic speeding past. The light turned to amber and then started to flash intermittently green. Did this mean he could cross? Cars reluctantly screeched to a halt, drivers tapping the steering wheel with obvious impatience. Before he knew, the green light started to flash red. The klaxon sounded and a voice annouced that his slot was over and he must not attempt to cross. The car that had stopped next to him at the intersection lowered its window.

Is this your idea of a joke? Don't you Peds realise that some of us have work to do?

He smiled apologetically and half raised a hand as an admission of guilt. Again the green light flashed. In his anxiety, he almost stepped in front of a car trying to and succeeding in beating it and, not for the first time that day, he had to stop and regulate his breathing before he felt sufficiently confident to walk the twenty yards to the front door of the King William IV Hotel. He opened it and stepped across the threshold. The door snapped shut behind him. He pulled the handle of the inner door. It appeared to be locked. After a moment, a whirring indicated that the locking mechanism had been released and when he pressed against the glass panel, the door swung open without effort.

What surprised him was how little the interior had changed. Originally the centrepiece of a thriving market, it had been patronised by well-to-do farmers and the professional classes. Over the years this status had gradually diminished but there had always been certain times of the day when it retained its former dignity. It was clear now that it had given up the unequal struggle and was the natural habitat of the flotsam and jetsam of all-day opening.

Bitter? No one drinks bitter. We sell lager—Super Premium, Premium or Regular.

He thought the last named would be safest, ordered a half and tried a joke:

Not many regulars about.

We don't encourage regulars. Only Peds drink in bars now.

As it was clear that the barman did not include small talk among his professional accomplishments, he decided to look for another source of information, perhaps the café. It was on his way to the door that he noticed a figure at the far end of the bar. Although the hair was thinner and the jowls had dropped, there was no doubt that it was Half a Lager Joe. Joe had earned this particular cognomen by drifting around the King Bill, keeping an eye on the state of any particular round. If he sensed a refill was imminent, he would attach himself to the group and squeeze into the conversation. When the drinks were reordered, he would, as often as not, find himself included and, with feigned surprise, would inevitably reply, 'If you must. Half a lager will do nicely.'

The King Bill was a very large pub and Joe's conversational contributions made up in variety what they lacked in substance. Thirty years ago a man to be avoided. Today to be claimed as a long lost friend. He moved towards that end of the bar. Joe, sensing his approach, looked up. His eyes first widened in recognition, then glazed as he tried to put a name to the face.

Hi! I didn't realise that you were still around.

I'm not. I'm just here for my Father's funeral.

He realised the 'just' was wrong but, in the welter of platitudes that followed, found it too late to explain.

More to the point, he needed Joe's advice to find the Crematorium. It was on the south side somewhere but he wasn't sure exactly where.

What's the best way to the Crem? Can I walk it?

Joe looked up as though a joke was being made at his expense.

The Crem's on South Side. You don't walk on South Side. Even they don't walk on South Side.

The term 'they' was accompanied by a slight sideways jerk of the head towards the surveillance camera that methodically swept the bar area.

That bad?

Joe nodded.

Bus then? Taxi?

Joe shook his head.

No call for them. The only people who would use them are Peds. Peds can't afford them. Ergo (the shard of a Grammar School education*) there ain't no buses, no taxis any more.*

He stopped, furrowed his brow and folded his hands as he had been wont to do in his days of dispensing professional advice.

Best hire a Bub—ten dollars an hour. There's an outlet next to KWIKSNAX. What time's the funeral?

In an hour. I'd better go.
Nice to see you. Mind the trams!

For some reason, Joe was much amused by this last remark and repeated it to himself several times while he sipped the accepted half of Premium.

The road was familiar but not known. There had been less difficulty than he had expected in hiring the car. ID checked. Money paid. A half-hearted attempt to persuade him to upgrade and he was carefully working his way through the one-way system that pointed to South Side. It was a very small car, not unlike the vehicle he was used to. This was a bit of luck as he had insisted that they let him go alone, by himself. At least, he thought that he had insisted. For a moment, he felt the panic of regret–it would have been easier if they had come. They said things had changed. Not many nice guys, Michael. You've got to look after yourself. But he was right to insist. It was important that he did it by himself. Suddenly he half saw the sign 'The Crematorium'–a further wave of relief and a sharp exhalation of breath. He glanced across to the passenger seat to check that his bag was safe.

As he turned on to the main road, he thought he

recognised the big houses. Although set back from the road, they were surprisingly visible. The protective hedgerows and shrubs had been torn down and the extensive gardens turned into half-hearted attempts at allotments. They had been worth a lot of money once. Wasn't it here that Charlie had the panscrub scam? Now they were virtually derelict, paint beyond peeling, windows blinded with boards. A noise started to penetrate his mind. At first he ignored it, assuming it was a return of the old trouble, but as it grew louder it formed the shape of a siren, persistent and demanding. In the rear mirror he could see the flashing lights and the psychedelic stripes against the white slab of the pursuing vehicle. It was travelling much, much faster than him. Even if he raced through the gears he was bound to get in the way. He must pull over, let it past.

This was easier thought than done. The side of the road was littered with abandoned, mostly wheelless cars, half-filled skips and what appeared to be a fabrication of wood and cardboard covered with barbed wire. Then a gap appeared and yellow lines loomed. Were cars allowed on them? How could they differentiate? Perhaps, it was pavement to road that activated the speaking machine. The siren became more strident, more insistent. He had to get out of the way. He knew it was often only a matter of minutes, even seconds, between life and death. Whether they died or were saved. He knew that all right. He swung into the gap, brushing a cardboard box, and half mounted the kerb. He jerked to a halt. The green, yellow and white ambulance streaked past. Then silence slowly fell.

His grip uncoiled on the steering wheel. He glanced in the mirror to see that the road was clear, selected reverse and, looking over his right shoulder, was about to back out. He was stopped by a tap on the passenger-side window. He turned his head 180 degrees and saw a face peering in. The face was different from the others he had seen that day. At first, he could not work out why. Then he realised–it was smiling. It was a face that was smiling. For some reason, for the first time since they had told him about his father's accident, he felt like crying but he smiled back and, leaning over, pressed the button that allowed the window to wind smoothly down.

Hi!

The left hand came through the aperture and

grasped the bag that was on the seat. As it was being pulled through the window, it jammed and he was able to make a desperate grab to attempt to retrieve it. He mustn't lose that—ID, travel-warrant and God knows what else were in it. Unexpectedly, he encountered no resistance and he pulled the bag back on to his lap to reveal the still smiling face. The left hand slipped from view and the right hand, previously invisible, thrust itself into the car.

Charlie Shearing was waiting for her to finish doing whatever she had to do and could have done half an hour before, so that they could go out. To pass the time, he flicked through the local paper where a news item caught his eye. After he had read it, he grimaced with that combination of a sniff and a shrug of the shoulders that indicates a sense of complacent superiority and shouted up to his wife:

You won't believe this. These Peds never learn. Some guy in a Bub got shot yesterday on South Side. Traffic Patrol say it seemed that he stopped on purpose. No sign of mechanical failure. Just pulled over at the side of the road. Pulled over in South Side for no reason.

Yes, darling. I'm sure you're right, darling. Be a sweetie and see if you can find my lighter.

There was a time when Charlie would have had his women running around after him, but things are not what they were. He eased himself out of the armchair and started, a slightly stooped figure, to search the room in a rather desultory manner.